SNOWFALL AT MOONGLOW

Snowfall at Moonglow

A Moonglow Christmas Novella

Deborah Garner

Cranberry Cove Press

Cranberry Cove Press
PO Box 1671
Jackson, WY 83001, United States

Library of Congress Catalog-in-Publication Data Available
Garner, Deborah
Snowfall at Moonglow / Deborah Garner—1st United States edition
1. Fiction 2. Woman Authors 3. Holidays

p. cm.
ISBN-13:
978-0-9969961-4-3 (paperback)
978-0-9969961-5-0 (hardback)

Printed in the United States of America
10 9 8 7 6 5 4 3 2

ONE

Mist stood on the front steps of the Timberton Hotel and looked up at the sky. It had been an odd December, warmer than usual despite a lack of sunshine. The possibility of snow seemed to whisper almost constantly from gray clouds above, teasing the small Montana town with hints of winter. Yet few snowflakes fell to the ground. Those that managed the journey dissipated before they could gather together into the white blanket that the holiday season longed for.

The creak of a door preceded footsteps behind her on the porch. Mist knew without looking that it was Betty. This year's Christmas guests had yet to arrive. Clive, Betty's beau, was the only other person often at the hotel, and he was at his gem gallery. Business had been brisk with the approaching holiday, especially for a small town. Word of Clive's custom sapphire jewelry had spread over the past few years.

"It's not looking like a white Christmas for our guests, is it?" Betty said. "They say a storm is coming, but I don't see any signs of one."

Mist turned as Betty stepped beside her, admiring the hotelkeeper's kind features and friendly disposition. She'd become a dear friend to Mist, almost like a mother. Their age difference was indeed that of mother and daughter, though Betty's short stature, round face, and soft curves bore no resemblance to Mist's willowy frame.

A soft breeze picked up, blowing a curtain of Mist's hair out of her french clip and into her face. She untangled a loose tendril from a dangling string of tiny seashells, a favorite necklace she'd had since her college days back in Santa Cruz, California.

"The snow will come," Mist said as she turned to go back inside.

"I hope you're right," Betty said, following her into the hotel. "Guests expect that at Christmas. They dream of it, just like Bing Crosby did."

Mist smiled, well aware of Betty's favorite Christmas tune. It was one of many they made sure to play for holiday guests. Nothing beat traditional music or food—or drinks for that matter. Christmas at the Timberton Hotel wasn't just any holiday gathering. It spoke of days gone by as well as days to come. It was a season of magic, and no two years were ever the same.

"Let me fix you some tea, Betty," Mist said. "Or some coffee, if you prefer." She entered the kitchen, Betty close behind her. Mist softly crossed the floor, her feet barely making a sound. She filled a teakettle with water and put it on the stove.

"Tea sounds good," Betty said, taking a seat at the kitchen's center table. "It's too late in the day for coffee. I need to get my beauty sleep." Smiling, she raised one hand to her gray hair, making a dramatic pouf motion.

"Cranberry scone?" Mist asked, lightly tapping a ceramic jar. "Fresh from this morning, you know."

Betty chuckled and patted a plump hip. "Indeed, I know. But I'd better work off the ones I already had first. Maybe I'll have one for dessert tonight."

"A good plan," Mist said. She set out two mugs and a variety of tea bags—chamomile, peppermint, lemon ginger, and cinnamon spice. She offered the assortment to Betty and then chose chamomile for herself.

"What's for dinner anyway?" Betty asked. She sniffed comically, as if trying to detect a clue. "Nothing in the oven yet, I take it."

This had become a daily guessing game of late as Mist had been pulling some surprise menus out of… well, her imagination it seemed. She was well-known for the mouthwatering food she served in the Moonglow Café, located on the ground floor of the hotel. Not only did the charming eatery feed overnight guests, but Betty and Mist could always count on a dozen or more townsfolk to show up at mealtime.

"Burritos," Mist said casually. An impish smile crossed her face as she fetched the teapot and poured boiling water into both cups.

Betty quirked an eyebrow as if unsure she had heard Mist correctly. "Burritos?" she repeated. "All right then. What a great idea, something simple that you can throw together at the last minute. Good for you, Mist. You spoil us with all the fancy dishes you serve."

Dipping her tea bag in and out of her cup, Mist smiled. Yes, there was fancy, and yes, there was simple. And then there was that great region of in-between, which could be a surprise in itself. She switched the subject to a more important matter at hand. "I was looking over the guest book earlier."

"I noticed we still have a few rooms available, unusual at Christmas time," Betty said.

Mist took a sip of her tea, an intricate silver ring on her index finger reflecting the overhead light as she lifted the mug to her mouth. She set it down gently and opened the reservation book. "The Professor will be here this year as long as he returns from England in time. I'm keeping his room open. He knows it will be available for him."

"I do hope he makes it by Christmas," Betty said. "But he did the right thing, going back to England to be with his mother while she's ill."

"Being with family and friends when they need us is always important," Mist said. "Clara and Andrew will definitely be here this year."

"And Michael, of course," Betty added with a wink.

Mist didn't need to see the wink. The hotelkeeper's teasing tone of voice gave it away. "He will be here," Mist said calmly, not taking the bait. Betty and Clive both enjoyed giving her a hard time about the growing romance between herself and Michael Blanton. Formerly a once-per-year Christmas guest, Michael had become more of a once-per-month guest, at times approaching weekly status.

"What do we know about this year's new guests?" Betty asked. "You took most of the reservations yourself."

Mist ran her finger down the printed list of rooms, noting the names next to each. "We have a mother and daughter arriving together, Allison and Kinsley Elliott."

"The ones from Indiana, right?"

"Yes, New Harmony." Mist almost whispered the name of the small town, so enchanting. "And Max Hartman, a businessman from New York, I believe." Mist frowned slightly.

"What is it?" Betty said, unnerved by an expression so contrary to Mist's nature.

Mist closed her eyes, inhaled slowly, exhaled, and finally opened her eyes again. "All will be well," she said. Moving on before Betty could ask questions, she slid her finger to another line. "Nina Pereira is coming all the way from Brazil."

"An international guest, how wonderful," Betty said. "It's always fascinating to learn about other countries and their customs."

Mist looked up at Betty and smiled. "This is how I know the snow will come."

"And why is that?" Betty chuckled. "Surely she's not bringing snow from Brazil."

"No, she is not," Mist said. "In fact, she's never seen snow before. She lives close to the Equator, in the Amazon rainforest."

Betty tilted her head to one side. "Maybe she's young and hasn't had a chance to travel."

"Eighty-seven."

"Eighty-seven what?" Betty took a sip of tea.

"She is eighty-seven years old," Mist said nonchalantly.

"Is she traveling alone?" Betty leaned forward, attempting to see any additional notes in the reservation book, but there were none.

"Yes, she will be alone. And she sounded quite proud of it when she called, which I found delightful."

"A bucket list trip perhaps." Betty proposed.

Mist nodded. "Exactly what she said."

"I'm envious," Betty said. "There are places I'd love to see. Paris, for instance."

"You and Clive should consider taking a trip," Mist said, looking up from the guest list.

Betty shook her head. "Clive has the gallery to run, and it wouldn't be right to leave you with the hotel on your own."

"Clive could close the gallery for a vacation," Mist said. "I can take care of the hotel. And Maisie and others would help, if needed."

"I'll think about it," Betty mused. "Back to the guest list."

"We'll make sure Ms. Pereira leaves here with cherished memories," Mist continued. Raising her hand into the air, Mist plucked an invisible memory and deposited it in an imaginary bucket on the counter.

"Sounds like a small group this year," Betty said. "A quiet holiday perhaps." She stood, took her teacup to the sink, and placed it in the basin. Taking a jacket from a coat rack by the kitchen's back door, she donned the outerwear and picked up a basket at the end of the counter. Knitting needles and colorful skeins of yarn peeked over the top.

Mist closed the reservation book and eyed the basket in Betty's hands. "Off to work on the Winter Warmth project with the other ladies? How is that going?"

Betty reached into the basket and held up a partial mitten in a deep purple hue.

"Maybe I should make a parmesan dish out of that," Mist said.

Betty looked at the unfinished mitten and laughed. It did resemble an eggplant more than a knitted accessory. "I see what you mean. I'd better get this over to Glenda before you coat it with bread crumbs and throw it in the oven."

"Glenda is adding all the thumbs, right?"

"Yes," Betty said. "She loves that part, so all mittens get passed to her when they're at that point. Millie, who has decades of knitting experience, adds the center design. And then Marge finishes off the cuffs. We're having so much fun. I can hardly wait to send them off with the warm jackets we've been gathering."

"What you're doing is wonderful, collecting clothing to provide warmth to those in need." Mist said. "And it's especially wonderful because you're all working on it together."

"It gives us a chance to visit. And to gossip a bit! Nothing hurtful, of course." Betty lowered her voice to a whisper even though no one else was around.

"Did you know Millie has a little flirtation going with another librarian up in Helena?"

Mist smiled. "I certainly didn't."

"You'd be amazed at the things I find out there," Betty said.

"I already am."

Mist waved to Betty as the hotelkeeper headed out, then carried her own teacup to the sink. She glanced at the wrought iron clock on the kitchen wall: two thirty, early enough to get a start on miniature paintings before preparing burritos—Moonglow-Café style, of course.

TWO

Mist closed the door to her room, a quiet space toward the end of a first-floor hallway that ran behind the kitchen, away from guest rooms. It served not only as sleeping quarters but as a studio for her artwork. In particular, at this time of year, miniature paintings took precedence over anything else. Not only had they become popular sellers in Clive's gallery—so much so that she could barely keep up with the demand—but Mist delighted in sending one home with each holiday guest. It had become an established tradition to present them to guests on Christmas morning.

Securing the tiny canvases on a custom easel that Clive had built for her, Mist looked over paint selections and laid out what she needed. Passing over colorful hues, she chose an unusually plain assortment for immediate use: light gray, a medium gray, white, and several shades that were just a tad off-white. She hesitantly added black but took it away, replacing it with a dark charcoal.

As was her habit, she stood back, folded her hands in front of her, and contemplated the blank canvases, waiting for them to give her instructions. This was her perception of the process, something she had felt since first staring at a blank sheet of paper as a child.

The empty space would summon its own design. All she had to do was be patient. The inspiration might approach from deep within her, from a wisp of wind, or from her visual surroundings. On this day, the latter stepped forward as surely as if the lightly overcast sky flowed through her window and brushed itself across her room. Envisioning the light gray clouds encircling the easel, she transferred their subtle shades onto each tiny canvas. After blending the softer shades together into a hazy background, she followed with circular swirls of white and off-white.

Stepping back, she tilted her head to one side and surveyed the overall effect. Satisfied, she cleaned up the paint supplies and returned to the kitchen. After all, she had a town to feed.

* * *

"Delicious!" "Exquisite!" "Dang-nab mouthwatering grub!"

The last of the compliments came from William Guthrie, better known as Wild Bill around town. His greasy-spoon café down the road, Wild Bill's, still served the occasional breakfast customer, but he was a true Moonglow Café fan when it came to his own meals.

"Never had burritos like this before." Wild Bill inspected the wrapped creation on his plate. "I'm not even sure what all I put in it, considering all those fancy dishes up there on the buffet."

"What *did* you put in it, Bill?" Clive asked. "You've got a mighty hefty concoction there." Never one to skip one of Mist's meals, Clive had closed the gallery just in time to slide in for dinner.

William Guthrie shrugged his shoulders. "Some of everything, I reckon." He held up the cumbersome burrito, which barely fit in his hand.

Mist, who was passing from table to table refilling water glasses, smiled. "Then I believe you have a *carne asada*, Jamaican jerk chicken, ginger tofu burrito with cilantro-lime quinoa, Cuban black beans, avocado-jalapeno salsa, mango-mint relish, and apple-corn compote in a sun-dried tomato-and-spinach tortilla."

Clayton, the town's fire captain, patted Bill on the back good-naturedly. "You're supposed to choose what you want to put in it."

"I believe he did exactly that," Mist said. "Not making choices *is* a choice."

"Spoken according to true Mist philosophy," Clive noted. Several others in the room nodded. Mist's reputation for having a new age viewpoint on life was well established.

"It looks like a red-and-green football, just a little misshapen," Clayton said. "You could probably pass that from here to Pop's Parlor in one long spiral. Not that I suggest trying," he added quickly as he saw Betty's brow furrow.

"Where'd you get these half-green and half-red tortillas anyway?" Clive asked.

"They're just two different batches of flour dough I made," Mist said. "Pressed together at the center before baking."

Wild Bill nodded with approval. "Very festive for the season, if I do say so myself. I believe I'll go short instead of long." With that, he lifted the burrito to his mouth and took a sizable bite.

The kitchen door swung open, and a spry young woman with purple streaks in her cropped hair entered. Maisie, Clayton's wife and the owner of Maisie's Daisies, held a serving tray with individual ramekins. Clay Jr. toddled behind her with a shaker of mixed cinnamon and sugar, a task cleverly assigned by his mother to allow him the satisfaction of helping.

"There you go, Bill," Clive said. "Mist's famous cinnamon raisin rice pudding, just in case that mountain of a burrito doesn't fill you up."

"I just might make myself another one and *still* have that rice pudding," Bill boasted. "This here is the dang finest burrito I ever had." Murmurs around the room showed others agreed with him.

"*Arroz con leche*," Mist clarified, giving the dessert a proper name for the theme of the meal. "It will be a sweet contrast to the bolder flavors of your dinner."

Maisie circled the room, offering dessert to those who wanted it, which turned out to be everyone. Clive waited until Mist turned away and then took two while holding a "don't tell" finger in front of his mouth, much to Maisie's amusement.

"I won't tell," Maisie whispered.

"*I* will," Bill said, causing Maisie to laugh out loud before he took a second ramekin himself.

"There's plenty to go around," Mist said, having slyly watched the whole scene play out. "We're a small group tonight."

"When do your guests arrive?" Clive asked as Betty entered from the kitchen. A spoonful of rice pudding hovered before Clive's mouth.

"Several arrive tomorrow," Betty said. "And the rest the next day." She glanced at Mist. "Do I have that right?"

Mist nodded. "Yes, exactly. Two days of arrivals, two days of holiday celebration, and two days releasing everyone back into the wild."

Bill chuckled. "You make it sound like you'll have a flock of geese here."

"Give 'em enough eggnog on Christmas Eve and it just might sound like it," Clive said, causing Bill to slap his leg and chuckle even louder. Clive joined in, as did Clayton, and soon the three men were guffawing it up together.

Betty and Maisie exchanged smirks, and Mist smiled as she headed back into the kitchen. The other two women followed closely behind.

"Men." Betty sighed, shaking her head. "Gotta love 'em."

"And love them we do," Maisie said. She set the empty dessert tray down on the center island and picked Clay Jr. up, cradling him against her hip. "Isn't that right? We love Daddy, don't we?" The toddler responded enthusiastically by jerking his head up and down.

"Speaking of men…" Betty hinted.

———

Maisie picked up on Betty's thoughts immediately and turned toward Mist. "Yes, when will Michael be here?"

"Tomorrow," Mist said. "He's at a faculty event tonight up in Missoula."

"A Christmas party, I bet," Maisie said. "How fun." She shuffled Clay Jr.'s position as he reached up and pulled a strand of purple hair, tugging it downward.

"A lecture, actually," Mist said. "Or perhaps it would be called a speech." She paused as if to consider the difference between the two descriptions. "Or a talk, I suppose," she added. "He's moderating a discussion of Charles Dickens' book *A Christmas Carol.*"

"Oh, I haven't read that in many years," Betty said. "You should have gone, Mist. I would have been happy to serve dinner tonight."

"Thank you, Betty." Mist sent a look of gratitude to the innkeeper. "But there's still more to do to prepare for the guests. For one thing, I need to make sure Maisie's Daisies has our flower order ready." She attempted an expression of mock concern but ended up smiling instead. She knew perfectly well that Maisie always managed to find exactly what she needed for her holiday decorations.

Maisie looked up at the ceiling and tapped her hand against her cheek as if considering whether or not her flower shop had remembered Mist's order. Clay Jr., mimicked the gesture by poking his mother's other cheek with a chubby finger.

"I also still need to add personal touches to the guest rooms."

"From your mystery closet," Betty noted.

"You have a mystery closet?" Maisie asked. "I didn't know that. It sounds, well, mysterious."

"Oh, it is," Betty said. "And she's been stashing new items in it this year. I peek in it now and then. You never know what you might find."

Mist looked at Betty and smiled, well aware that the hotelkeeper looked at her collection of random trinkets and treasures periodically. It pleased her to know her ever-changing assortment drew Betty's curiosity.

"Great dinner," Clive said as he entered the kitchen. "Almost like one of your art projects, Mist, getting to pick and choose what to put in those burritos." He sauntered over to Betty and gave her a peck on the cheek.

"Thank you, Clive," Mist said. "Very kind of you to say."

Betty laughed as she put an arm around Clive's waist. "Every now and then his manners slip out."

"In spite of myself," Clive added, going along with Betty's gentle teasing. "As a matter of fact, I feel so well-mannered tonight that I just might help with the dishes."

"And you'll even use soap?" Betty quipped.

"Sure thing. I'll go grab a bar from the shower." He winked at Mist and then headed for the sink where a stack of plates demanded attention. To no one's surprise, he picked up the liquid dish detergent, turned on the water, and started in.

"I'd better get this little ragamuffin home to bed," Maisie said. She bid the group good night and left, Clay Jr. still in her arms.

"I'll help Clive," Betty said, directing her statement to Mist. "You go ahead and relax. Or use the time for your projects."

"Like more of your miniature paintings for the gallery?" Clive hinted. "The ones with the winterberries have been in particular demand this year. And those snowmen. Come to think of it, a few more of the pine trees would be good too."

"Clive!" Betty exclaimed. "Mist has guests arriving tomorrow."

Mist smiled. "It's just fine, Betty. I have an assortment prepared and set aside." She shifted her comments to Clive, a sly grin on her face. "After several years making the paintings for the gallery, I'm familiar with your sweetheart's *advance* ordering system. I'll drop them off tomorrow."

"Is that actual sarcasm I'm hearing from Mist?" Clive said.

"And well deserved," Betty quipped as she nudged Clive gently with her elbow.

Mist returned to the café room and brought the leftovers from the buffet back into the kitchen. She filled an individual reusable container with an assortment of burrito makings and wrapped several tortillas to go with it. The rest she placed in the kitchen's oversized refrigerator before turning to Betty and Clive, who were joking and laughing while washing dishes.

"You two look like you have things under control. I'm going to drop this off and then ponder a few details for our incoming guests."

Betty glanced at the container in Mist's hands and smiled. "You take good care of him," she said, referring to Hollister. The town's formerly homeless man kept to himself but now lived downstairs in Room 7.

"She takes good care of us all," Clive added.

"We take care of each other," Mist said. "As it should be." With that, she slipped out of the kitchen silently, content in the knowledge that some of her favorite projects lay ahead.

THREE

Morning dawned bright and sunny without a hint of snow in the air. Beams of light flowed into the café as a dozen or so townsfolk enjoyed an herbed frittata with potato pancakes and fresh berries. As always, java love, Mist's personal name for coffee, filled mugs. A woven basket rested on a table near the door with the words *Pay what your heart tells you* in rustically artistic calligraphy. This, the only price given for any meal at the Moonglow Café, always managed to cover the cost of feeding everyone.

"Still hoping for snow," Betty mused. She looked out the kitchen window as she dried dishes from the breakfast meal.

"The snow will come," Mist said, just as she'd said before.

"Somehow I believe you," Betty said.

"Believing is a good thing," Mist said. "And right now I believe I need to go add a few finishing touches to the rooms."

"Ah, your closet," Betty said.

"The realm of the unknown," Mist quipped, impishly imitating herself. She left Betty to finish up the last of the dishes and glided down the hallway behind the kitchen until she arrived at the closet. Before opening the door, she ran her hand over the surface, admiring the grain of the wood in the same way a reader might caress the cover of a just-finished book. Pleased with the smooth texture, she opened the door.

Mist gathered the rayon folds of her midcalf-length skirt together and lowered herself to the closet floor, settling into a comfortable position. Looking around at the baskets, boxes, and shelves, she felt certain she could personalize each guest room with odds and ends she'd collected during the past year. In fact, not all the closet's contents were items she'd collected on her own. By now, others knew of her eclectic collection kept in the not-so-secret-anymore hideaway. Millie, the town librarian, dropped off books now and then. Sally, owner of the local thrift shop, Second Hand Sally's, had adopted a habit of setting aside unique donations for Mist to see before putting them out to sell. And former guests had even taken to sending an oddity on occasion, having been charmed by whatever they'd found in their room on a particular holiday stay.

In spite of preferring a somewhat haphazard splash of items, Mist had organized the closet over the past few months. A two-drawer oak file cabinet that she'd found at a yard sale held folders of cards, photographs, poems, and printed articles. This prevented damage by clunky objects—an antique toy fire truck, for example—that might land on something more delicate—say, an onionskin love letter mailed from Paris during WWII.

A compartmentalized acrylic box held dollhouse miniatures she'd gathered over the years, tiny furniture, appliances, and décor. She'd made an exceptionally exciting find only recently: a full set of English holiday china and silverware, no single piece too large to balance on the tip of her finger. It had taken four of the twenty-four compartments just to hold the set.

A weekend trip to an antique store in Helena had led to the old trunk against the back side of the closet, which held fabric, yarn, and miscellaneous sewing knickknacks. Even with the current mitten project going on, Mist had managed to hide away a skein of heather-gray merino wool as well as one in a deep raspberry shade with mixed alpaca and silk fibers. Without looking inside the trunk, she knew the two skeins rested comfortably on a pile of Battenberg lace doilies, bundles of fabric remnants piled on either side.

Mist shifted her weight, tucked her legs to one side, and leaned against a stuffed llama that greeted her each time she opened the closet door. She'd adopted the fluffy camel cousin on a trip to Missoula earlier in the fall when she'd found him smiling at her from a garage sale driveway. For the modest fee of fifty cents, she'd gathered him into her arms, named him Soft—not Softy or Softly or Soft Stuff, just Soft—and driven him safely to his new home in Timberton.

"What do you suggest, Soft?" Mist asked. Not expecting an answer, she paused anyway, listening to the silence offer possibilities. "Yes, books, of course… and toys… memory prompts. Bright colors, subdued shapes—fine ideas." She patted Soft's chest appreciatively. "I agree." She stood and gathered specific items as metal hinges creaked.

"Are you talking to Soft again?" Betty's voice was both kind and teasing as she peeked around the edge of the closet door.

"Yes, but not too softly," Mist quipped, tossing back the newly formed banter she and Betty had developed after adding Soft to the household.

"Any answers?"

"A few," Mist said as she pulled a pink satin ribbon from a square wicker basket, draped it over one shoulder, and stood up. "It's often possible to find answers in silence." As if cued by her own words, she gathered additional chosen items into her arms and stepped out into the hallway. She closed the door with one tap of a ballet-shoed foot, smiled as Betty returned to the kitchen, and began the ritual of distributing the odds and ends.

Just after finishing with the last upstairs room and returning downstairs, the chime of bells from the front door signaled the arrival of the first guests. Mist crossed the hotel lobby, wondering if she was about to greet Max Hartman, but found Allison and Kinsley Elliott on the front porch instead. To both her relief and concern, she felt herself relax. It was unlike her to feel apprehensive about a guest's arrival, but she hadn't been able to shake the disturbing feeling she'd had when Mr. Hartman had first called.

"Welcome to the Timberton Hotel," Mist said as she ushered the mother and daughter inside. She stepped aside so the two willowy figures could pass by. Each wore similar styles of coats, almost identical in color, and their scarves and hats were the same. Although their heights were different—Allison, the mother, standing a full foot taller than her daughter—they looked almost like twins. Both sported brown hair pulled back into a braid, and they wore matching silver hoop earrings. Kinsley looked to be in tween years but not by much. Perhaps ten, Mist mused. The young girl had an appearance that might indicate an age anywhere from eight to twelve. Both faces were scrubbed clean and makeup-free.

"Let me take your coats," Mist offered. She hung them on a coatrack in the corner of the entryway and turned back to the new arrivals, ready to get them situated. Before she could offer them anything, the front door opened. A loud male voice accompanied the sound of footsteps scraping the doormat outside as cold air blew in.

"Sell forty shares of it and buy the other." A fifty-something man stepped inside, cell phone in hand. He switched the phone from one ear to the other as he shook off his jacket. Before Mist could offer to take it, he stepped between her and the other arrivals and hung it up himself. "Absolutely not," he said, continuing his conversation without so much as a nod of greeting to anyone. "Yes, immediately, and tell Peterson to get cracking on the Murray investment. *Today*, not tomorrow or next week or next year. Report back." He ended the call and immediately made another. "Thompson, run that transfer through that we talked about..." He moved into the front parlor and took a seat.

Mist turned her attention back to Allison and Kinsley. "I have a registration card for you to fill out, but perhaps you'd like some hot cocoa, coffee, or tea first? You've traveled a long way."

Kinsley's eyes brightened. She opened her mouth to answer, but her mother spoke first. "Maybe later. We'd like to get settled in first."

"Of course." Mist smiled, shifting her attention from mother to daughter and then back to the mother. She led them to the registration desk, let them fill out and sign the card, and then escorted them to their room upstairs. Allison and Kinsley each carried a suitcase. "This is one room, but it's actually a suite," Mist pointed out upon arriving at the accommodation. "There's a door against the far wall that I've left unlocked. No one is booked for the second room, so you're welcome to use it. Perhaps Kinsley would like her own room, since it's connected to yours."

"There are two beds in this one," Allison said. "This will be fine for both of us."

Mist felt certain she saw a brief expression of longing cross the daughter's face, which disappeared just as quickly. "I'll let you two relax," Mist said. She pointed out amenities around the room and repeated the offer of drinks, as well as Betty's glazed cinnamon nuts. Every Christmas, a crystal bowl of the sweet treats sat on the registration desk at all times.

Returning downstairs, Mist glanced in the front parlor, hoping to be able to greet the other new arrival, clearly Max Hartman. Both the man's voice and countenance were recognizable from his initial phone call to make the reservation. She'd been placed on hold at least five times during that call. Finding him engrossed in another long-distance conversation, she headed for the kitchen instead, where she found Betty spooning cookie dough onto a greased cookie sheet.

"I thought I'd get these cinnamon cookies done before you need the kitchen again." Betty scooped the last round of dough onto the sheet and slipped the cookies into the oven. Others already sat cooling on a wire rack.

"Preparing for the big event?" Mist knew the answer. Betty's annual cookie exchange was one of the highlights of the season, along with Mist's much-loved Christmas Eve dinner.

"Yes," Betty said. "I can hardly wait to see what kind of cookies and goodies the others bring. Needless to say, neither can Clive."

Both Mist and Betty laughed, knowing Clive would be the first to sneak around. He prided himself with being an official taste-tester.

"I believe Marge is bringing fudge," Mist said.

"Yes." Betty nodded. "She was whipping up a batch when I stopped by the candy store yesterday afternoon."

"Let me guess," Mist said, smiling. "You just happened to drop in for some caramels?" The question was meant in jest. Betty's addiction to caramels was legendary.

"And Millie is bringing peanut butter cookies," Betty said. "It's her cousin Petrenia's recipe."

"I'm sure we'll have a good variety, as always. I might even whip something up to contribute."

"You already made papier mâché baskets for us." Betty pointed out a collection on the end of the main kitchen counter. "The pine cone and evergreen designs you painted on them are wonderful."

"Thank you, Betty," Mist said. "That's nice of you to say so. But you know that kind of project is fun for me. Your cookie exchange just gave me a good excuse to make them."

Betty nodded in the direction of the front parlor. "I take it that loud voice is associated with the frown I saw on your face when reading the guest list to me."

Mist sighed and remained quiet.

"That tough?" Betty quirked an eyebrow.

"Only to find words to match my thoughts," Mist said.

"Do you think we're going to have a problem with this guest?" Betty tapped her fingers on the kitchen countertop.

"No," Mist said, not hesitating. "I don't think we'll have a problem at all. But he may have a problem with us." She closed her eyes briefly, as if thinking over her statement, and then opened them again.

"Well, he chose to come here," Betty pointed out.

Mist shook her head. "Actually, he didn't. It was arranged for him as some kind of corporate gift."

"He could have said no." Betty shrugged her shoulders.

"Yes, he could have," Mist said. "But he felt obligated to accept it. The phone conversation I had with him was odd. Still, it is good that he's here. Hopefully, it will be good for the other guests."

"Hopefully?" Betty repeated.

"Energy flows between all living things." Mist took a deep breath, exhaled, and smiled. "We may just have to direct the flow a little."

FOUR

"I believe I smell chocolate!" Clive exclaimed as he stepped into the kitchen.

"All the way from your gallery?" Betty fought to keep a straight face. "Almost two blocks away?"

Clive grinned. "Well, maybe I just moseyed on down here *in case* something smelled tempting."

"Seeing as it's the day before the cookie exchange, you mean," Betty said, chuckling.

"Exactly." Clive laughed as he gave Betty a peck on the cheek and swiped a cookie from the cooling rack. "I felt optimistic about the timing. It might have been ESP."

Mist and Betty both smiled. It didn't take extrasensory perception to know there was a likelihood of cookies being baked the day before the annual cookie exchange.

"I think I heard a car pull up," Betty said. She glanced at the kitchen clock and quickly dried her hands on a holly-patterned towel. "I bet that's Clara and Andrew."

"Yes," Mist agreed. "Clara said they'd be here about this time. Their rooms are both ready. I put Clara's favorite quilt in hers and a collection of travel books in Andrew's."

"That's right," Betty said. "Her last postcard mentioned they were hoping to plan trips for next year. Didn't they just return from one? I can't remember." Gesturing for Clive to follow, Betty and Mist headed for the front lobby, reaching it just as Clara and Andrew entered. A chilly but snowless rush of air followed them in.

"Clara!" Betty exclaimed as she hugged the woman. "It's so good to see you again. As well as you," she added, turning toward Andrew, who was shaking hands with Clive.

"Thanks," Andrew said. He finished greeting Clive and gave Betty a friendly hug.

"We missed you guys last year," Betty said. "So glad you were able to be here this time." She clapped her hands, causing Mist to smile.

"Yes, we did," Mist said as Clara pulled her into an embrace. "And we have your rooms ready for you. Let me take your coat, hat, and gloves." She held out both hands as Clara handed over her outerwear. Hanging the coat, she placed the hat and gloves on a side table.

"Clive will be happy to help with your luggage, of course," Betty added, giving Clive a nudge in the ribs.

Andrew shook his head. "Not necessary, but thank you, Clive. We only have two bags, and I can carry them."

"Oh, and about the rooms…," Clara said as she fought back a grin. Not only was she not successful, but she collapsed into giggles.

"Are you all right, Clara?" Betty asked, eyebrows raised.

Mist spoke up, smiling. "I believe she's just fine."

"Well, I don't know about that," Andrew said, grinning. "It's possible she's lost her mind. Otherwise, she's fine." He wrapped an arm around Clara's shoulders and pulled her close.

Betty crossed her arms and tapped one foot, imitating a stern mother facing a couple of teenagers. "What am I missing here?"

"Well," Clara said, only half recovered from her fit of giggles. "We won't be needing both rooms."

"All right," Betty said, uncrossing her arms. "That's fine."

"Well?" Clara leaned forward and whispered to Betty. "Aren't you going to ask us why?"

"It would hardly be appropriate to question that!" Betty whispered back.

"Oh, for crying out loud," Clive said. "What's all this giggling and whispering about anyway?"

"I believe it's about this," Mist said. She reached forward and lifted Clara's left hand, allowing the overhead light to reflect off a row of channel-set diamonds in an elegant gold band.

Betty gasped. "You got married? How wonderful! We want details! When was the wedding? When was it? Who was there? Where was it held?"

"What wedding?" Andrew said as Clive gave him a congratulatory slap on the back. "We eloped!"

"Just three days ago!" Clara added. She looked at Andrew and beamed. He returned the same devoted look.

———

"Well, what do you know?" Clive said, nodding with approval. "Newlyweds here for Christmas. What a great way to spend your first married holiday together."

"Exactly what we thought," Clara said, her eyes sparkling.

Betty turned to Mist, eyebrows raised. "Did you know about this?"

Mist shook her head. "Not until Clara handed me her gloves a few minutes ago. I saw the ring when she took them off."

"Well, I say this calls for a celebration!" Clive said, turning to Betty and Mist. "Do you ladies have any of that fancy bubbly stuff around?"

"I believe we do," Betty said, heading to the kitchen to fetch a bottle of champagne.

"Yes," Mist confirmed, turning back to the newlyweds. "Maybe you'd like to settle in and then join us down here? Between the two accommodations you have booked, I suggest Clara's room. It's a little larger and gets wonderful light. The quilt is lovely too."

"Oh, yes!" Clara said. "I love that beautiful cathedral star pattern with all the holiday colors. I fell in love with that quilt the first time I saw it."

"Lead the way," Andrew said. Grasping the two suitcases after turning down another offer of help from Clive, he followed Clara up the stairs. Mist and Betty returned to the kitchen.

"Who's that man pacing outside on the sidewalk?" Clive asked. "I noticed him when Clara and Andrew entered. He was waving one arm around and had a cell phone pressed to his ear with the other." He attempted to grab a cookie, but Betty swatted his hand away.

"He's one of our guests this year," Betty said as she blocked access to the cooling rack of cinnamon cookies. "I believe his name is Mr. Hartman. Isn't that right?" She directed the question to Mist.

"Yes," Mist said. "I'm quite sure that's who it is."

"You're quite sure? Isn't he registered under his name?" Clive made another unsuccessful attempt to swipe a cookie.

"He hasn't registered yet," Mist said. "He's been occupied with phone calls. But I recognize his voice."

"From when he called to make the reservation," Betty added, seeing the confusion on Clive's face. "Mist spoke with him then."

Clive rubbed his chin. "Well, he certainly seems… as we used to say… *uptight*."

"When people lead a hectic life on a daily basis, it can be difficult to wind down and relax," Mist said.

"He'll come around once he gets involved with activities here, I'm sure," Betty said.

"Yes, involved…," Mist mused. "Come to think of it, I have a very heavy order to pick up at Maisie's Daisies. I think I'll head there now."

"I didn't realize flowers were heavy, but I'll be happy to help." Clive started toward his coat, which was hanging on a hook near the kitchen's back door.

"Thank you, Clive, but not this time," Mist said as she grabbed a forest green cape from the same area.

"I believe I'll have enough help for this particular trip. You and Betty go enjoy the champagne with Clara and Andrew." She wrapped the cape around her shoulders and smiled as she slipped out of the kitchen and headed for the front sidewalk.

FIVE

A few soft gray clouds hovered above as Mist stepped out of the hotel and descended the front steps. Tufts of snow left over from the week before dotted the ground to each side of the walkway, just enough to verify the time of year but not enough to form the white blanket that visitors dreamed of. Mist sent silent wishes into the air in hopes the weather forecast of a storm would be realized.

Max Hartman looked up from a phone call as Mist approached. He covered the cell phone with his free hand and asked if he could help her, just as she expected. She knew any business-trained person would do the same thing, often expecting a polite *no* in return. Thus the courtesy would be extended and fulfilled quickly and properly and business could continue uninterrupted.

"Yes, I would love some help," Mist said, well aware this was not the answer Mr. Hartman was hoping for.

"Sorry, but I have to finish this call," Mr. Hartman said, feigning—or so Mist surmised—disappointment that he wouldn't be able to help with whatever request she had.

"That's no problem at all," Mist said, and he nodded in a predictably courteous manner. Much to his surprise, she added, "I'll be glad to wait." She folded her hands in front of her and leaned against the sturdy brick column that held the hotel's mailbox. Mr. Hartman paced away and then back again, only a few short phrases clear enough to hear. "Yes, overnight express!" "Insist on fifteen days." "Not acceptable."

If Mist had been wearing a watch—she never did, feeling time to be fluid—she would have estimated the call to continue another ten minutes. And the next call—Mr. Hartman held up his index finger to indicate one more—another five. Finally, done with immediate business, he slipped his phone into a pocket and turned to Mist. "How may I help you?"

"We haven't had a chance to meet yet," Mist began. "I believe you're Max Hartman. My name is Mist. We spoke when you called to make your reservation." She reached out to shake his hand, and he perfunctorily returned the gesture.

"Misty, is it?"

"No, just Mist."

"Well then, how can I help you?"

Mist smiled in a way that might have seemed patronizing coming from anyone else. From her, it appeared to be more of a calculated expression to break the ice. For extra measure, she tilted her head slightly to the side. A slender silver earring with a dangling crystal of rose quartz brushed her shoulder.

"I need to pick up an order just down the street." She gestured in one direction with her arm, and the two began to walk. "What is your favorite flower, Mr. Hartman? In the winter, that is."

"Call me Max, and my favorite… just a moment." The man pulled his phone out in response to an abrasive ringtone. He looked at the caller ID, hit Decline and put the phone away. "You were asking… my favorite flower? Is that what you asked?" His expression told her he was sure he'd misheard.

"For winter," Mist clarified. She clasped the front of her cape and pulled it together as a gust of wind kicked up. "Your favorite winter flower."

"I don't have one."

"Pick one anyway."

"Those, I guess." The man pointed to a row of poinsettias outside Pop's Parlor. Mist remembered Ernie, the night bartender, ordering them from Maisie a few weeks before. Some of the regulars had ribbed him about the display. But the traditional holiday plant added color to the frontage of the otherwise-drab local watering hole.

"Poinsettias, nice," Mist mused. "Personally, I like red dendrobium."

"Red what?"

"Dendrobium. Such a lovely orchid. And parrot tulips, white, especially." Mist waved to Marge as she passed the candy shop, then indicated their destination on the other side of the street: Maisie's Daisies.

"Quaint little town," Max said as he looked around, his tone reflecting neither compliment nor criticism.

"Yes." Mist chose not to comment further, letting him draw his own impressions. Instead, she stepped inside the flower shop. Max entered just behind her.

Maisie emerged from the back room, summoned by the bell on the shop's front door. She wore a white sweatshirt that had seen better days and overalls dusted with potting soil. A twig jutted out of her purple-streaked hair, one sole leaf dangling from the end. "There you are," she said. "I was getting ready to bring your order over to the hotel."

"No need," Mist replied with a sly smile. "Mr. Hartman here was kind enough to offer to come pick them up."

"How wonderful," Maisie said, turning her attention to Max. "Mist works so hard to make the holidays perfect for all of us. It's always nice to see her get help."

"My pleasure," Max said, both awkwardly and formally.

"Give me just a minute. I'll bring everything out." Maisie disappeared into the back, and Max took advantage of the break to pull out his phone and send a brief text. Maisie soon returned with a large cardboard carton. Tiny tips of evergreens rose an inch or two above the top, approximately a dozen altogether. She placed the carton on the counter. "I just finished repotting them individually."

Mist reached into the box and pulled out a tiny tree about six inches tall. It rose from a basic plastic pot not unlike those that could be found at any garden center.

"They'll need to be watered," Maisie pointed out. "I suggest early in the day, giving them time to drain before putting them on the tables."

"Good advice." Mist laughed, imagining water seeping toward guests' place settings during the elegant Christmas Eve dinner.

Maisie stepped around the counter and lifted the box into Max's arms. "Let me get the rest." She disappeared into the back again, emerging with a gigantic vase of Queen Anne's Lace, which Mist took in her arms. "These have a vase life of three to seven days, even longer if cared for properly. I'll stop by tomorrow to cut the stems and add fresh water and floral preservative. They'll be fine for Christmas Eve."

"Perfect," Mist said, admiring the tiny white flowers. "So delicate, like snowflakes."

"Then you'll have snowflakes whether the storm comes in or not," Maisie said, "at least inside the hotel."

"The snow will come," Mist said, setting the potted tree back in the carton with the others.

Maisie held the door open so she and Max could carry the order out. "I'll see you at the cookie exchange. Tell Betty I'm bringing lemon nut bars. I've had to hide them from Clayton and Clay Jr., just so they won't disappear before I have a chance to share them."

Mist laughed. "I imagine there are cookies hidden all over town."

"I can't wait to see what you do with these," Maisie said, indicating the small trees. "Quite a change from the fancy array of flowers you've ordered other years."

Mist thanked her and followed Max, who had already stepped outside. Looking back at Maisie, she smiled. "Sometimes change is the most important order of all."

The short walk back was uneventful, aside from one delay while Max set the carton of small evergreen trees down on a bench to check another incoming call. Seeing a new car pulling up in front of the hotel, Mist gestured in that direction. Not receiving an acknowledgment from Max, she continued on her own, holding the vase of flowers close to protect it from the wind. She reached the car just as the driver's door opened.

"So, this is the Timberton Hotel," a lightly accented voice murmured as a woman stepped out of the car. She stood no more than five feet tall and hardly appeared to weigh more than the flowers Mist held in her arms. Her light gray hair was cut short in a practical style that spoke of ease and efficiency. She wore a light winter coat and fur-lined boots, both obviously new.

"You must be Nina Pereira." Mist shifted the vase in her arms to offer her hand in greeting.

"I am," Nina said. She shook Mist's hand, opened the back door of the rental car, and pulled a suitcase from the back seat, which Mist offered to take.

"I can carry it," Nina said, adding herself to the list of guests who were taking care of their own luggage.

"You've had a long trip, all the way from Brazil," Mist said. "We're delighted you're here to spend Christmas with us."

"I read about your hotel and café online and knew it was the perfect place for winter," Nina said. "And

I see…" Her voice trailed off as she looked around, both pleased and disappointed. "You have a little snow."

"More will be coming," Mist assured her. "A storm is moving in tonight."

"Welcome," Betty called, having just stepped out on the front porch. Seeing the vase of flowers in Mist's arms, she escorted Nina inside.

"We have a lovely first-floor room for you," Mist said. With her one free arm, she set a registration card and pen on the counter.

"Very convenient for sneaking out at night for treats here in the lobby," Betty added, pointing out the bowl of glazed cinnamon nuts.

"Those look tempting!" Nina said. "I may just have to enjoy one or two."

"Or three or four," Betty suggested. Both she and Nina laughed.

The sound of the front door opening was followed by Max's rapid entrance, the carton of evergreens in his arms. "Where should I put these?" he asked, his cell phone adding a muffled ringtone from his coat pocket.

"Excuse me, Nina," Mist said, turning toward Max. "A table in the café would be great. Thank you."

"I'll show you to your room," Betty said, lifting a key from a hook behind the registration desk. "Mist seems to have her hands full." She turned back to Mist and winked as she added, "With flowers, of course."

SIX

Closing the café doors for privacy and concentration, Mist took a look in the evergreen carton and then surveyed the room. The miniature trees, no more than seedlings, were exactly what she'd envisioned, and she felt grateful that Maisie had been able to bring them in. Potted carefully for interim use as decorations, she and Betty had plans for them after the holidays.

Moving from one table to the next, she placed a pot on each table that seated two to four people and three down the center of a long table for twelve, choosing shorter trees for the dining tables so that guests would be able to see each other. She placed the taller trees along the buffet. Once she added special touches, those would form a backdrop for the Christmas Eve feast.

"How do the little trees look?" Betty asked as she slipped into the café. She closed the door behind her and looked around.

"Quite lovely, I think," Mist said, stepping back to take in the overall effect.

"This was a wonderful idea," Betty said, "using live saplings for centerpieces so we can plant them for the New Year. And they look beautiful just as they are, simple against the wooden tables. But I suspect that's not your plan."

Mist moved to a nearby tree and touched the branches softly, as if caressing the pine needles. "Yes and no. We will keep them simple yet also add a touch of the winter that guests are hoping for."

Betty nodded. "I'm sure you have something wonderful planned."

"For dinner?" Clive's voice startled both Betty and Mist, who hadn't noticed him stick his head into the room.

"Not everything is about food," Betty chided.

"Maybe to Clive it is," Mist said, smiling. "But dinner is hours away. There's banana-nut bread in the kitchen if you feel you need sustenance at this very moment."

"Music to my ears!" Clive grinned and disappeared.

Betty laughed as she headed for the kitchen door. "I'll go make sure he doesn't eat the whole loaf."

Mist turned her attention back to the small trees, thinking over the eclectic variety of additions she intended to use to create a snowy scene on each table. After all, if the snow didn't manage to arrive outside, she'd simply have to bring it inside, at least in the guests' imagination. Between the Queen Anne's Lace, soft white chiffon she'd already set aside, tiny sparkling lights, and sweet—in fact, downright delicious—snowflakes, the guests would be able to enjoy their holiday meal while enjoying a winter wonderland. For tonight, she'd wrap a red satin ribbon around the base of each tree. Simple centerpieces would do for now. Their transformation would come later.

With that in mind, Mist carried the vase of flowers into the kitchen and placed it on a side counter. She found Betty at the center kitchen island, seated beside Clive.

"How was the banana-nut bread?" Mist asked, noting an empty plate with crumbs on the countertop in front of Clive.

"Delicious, of course," Clive said. "Perfect with Betty's coffee." He lifted a mug in the air as if making a toast. "Between the two of you, I'm a happy guy."

"And don't you forget it." Betty laughed.

"Not a chance," Clive said. "I count my blessings every day."

"Oh…" Betty turned to Mist, a worried look on her face. "Allison just informed me she and her daughter are both vegan. Will this be a problem for Christmas Eve dinner? Can you work something in for them? I know you have the menu planned already."

"And we're right back to 'what's planned for dinner,'" Clive quipped. Both Betty and Mist ignored him, knowing he was just giving them a bad time.

"It won't be a problem at all," Mist said. "We always have vegan options. It's important to have something for everyone, especially when we have a large buffet and crowd."

Clive harrumphed. "Well, I'll tell you right now I'm not eating a plain bowl of lettuce for Christmas Eve dinner."

"That's a good thing," Mist said with mock relief, "because there won't *be* a plain bowl of lettuce on the buffet." She and Betty exchanged amused grins.

Clive furrowed his brow, playing into the discussion. "But you'd *get* me the bowl of lettuce if I asked for it, right?"

"I'd have to think about it…" Mist teased. Both Betty and Clive laughed. "Oh, by the way"—Mist continued—"how did you like that lasagna I served last week?"

"Delicious!" Clive exclaimed. "You had me worried when you said it had spinach and mushrooms in it, but it was fantastic!"

"Glad to hear that," Mist said. "What about that frittata with the sun-dried tomatoes and basil the other morning? With the pecan waffles and maple syrup to go with it?"

Clive nodded his head enthusiastically. "I'm hoping you'll make that whole meal again soon." He turned to Betty. "They say breakfast is the most important meal of the day, you know. That's why I make sure I'm here early."

"That banana-nut bread you just had wasn't bad either, was it?" Mist tilted her head in the direction of the freshly sliced loaf.

"It was so good I broke down and had two pieces," Clive said. He grinned and patted his stomach for emphasis.

"*Three*," Betty whispered.

"I've gotta get back to the gallery. I can only get away with that Back in ten minutes sign for so long."

Clive stood up and took his coffee mug to the sink. "Why are you asking me all this anyway?"

Mist smiled, a twinkle in her eye. "Just curious."

Clive grabbed his jacket, gave Betty a peck on the cheek, and headed out.

"His sales are up this year, aren't they?" Mist said.

"Yes," Betty said. "His jewelry and your paintings are both selling well. Even the business from drop-in customers searching gravel for Yogo sapphires is up. Every year the place does a little better."

"The combination of art, jewelry, and gems is fascinating," Mist said. "And visitors get to learn about Montana sapphire mining when they visit Clive's gallery as well."

"He does love to tell people about the history of the area," Betty said. "It's a little like visiting a museum there, isn't it?"

"Absolutely," Mist agreed. "And people love watching him make the jewelry. Speaking of which, I wonder what ornament he's giving you this year."

"How do you know he has an ornament for me?" Betty laughed, knowing Mist's forthcoming answer.

"Because he makes one for you each year," Mist said. "He has for the past four years, I know. So far you have... let me think... a Christmas tree, a star..."

"A wreath, and a reindeer," Betty said to finish recounting the collection so far.

"Each with at least one tiny Yogo sapphire in it somewhere," Mist added. "They're wonderful, especially since Clive creates them himself. Handmade gifts are always special."

A phone call interrupted the conversation, and Betty picked up the cordless phone they always kept nearby. After a few words of greeting, she passed the phone to Mist. "For you."

Mist took the phone, spoke for a few minutes, and ended the call with a smile.

"You're beaming. Let me guess," Betty said. "Michael's on his way."

"Yes," Mist said. "And he's bringing the Professor with him."

"Wonderful," Betty exclaimed. "I didn't think Michael would be here until tomorrow, or Nigel, for that matter. Better known to us as the Professor, of course."

"It seems Nigel took an earlier flight from England and got in today," Mist said. "With the storm predicted, they decided to drive down now. They'll be here tonight."

"In time for dinner?"

"No," Mist said. "But in time for a late dessert in front of the fireplace. And tea for the Professor, naturally. I have his favorite, PG Tips, ready for him."

"This is perfect," Betty said. "We'll have all our guests here and settled in by tonight. It's going to be a lovely holiday. Now we just need the snow to arrive."

"The snow will come," Mist said. A sudden mischievous look crossed her face. "And I have just the activity to celebrate its arrival."

"What have you got up your sleeve now?" Betty said, leaning forward as if expecting a secret to be revealed.

Mist smiled. "Let's just wait for the snow to arrive."

SEVEN

Achilly wind swept into Timberton not long after Clive returned to the gallery. Mist put the makings of a hearty stew in a large pot to simmer and set dinner rolls to rise in two towel-covered pans. Moving to the front parlor, she nodded hello to Max Hartman, who hovered over his laptop. She then peered out the large window that framed the hotel's Christmas tree. The late afternoon sun was merely orange haze behind an overcast sky that had been growing darker for several hours. Mist knew without even stepping outside that the sensation of approaching snow would be heavy in the air.

Turning to the tree—a stately six-footer this year—she admired the old-fashioned ornaments that adorned the branches. Every year, a few new ones showed up, whether something whimsical that Mist found at a crafts fair or a handmade creation by one of the local children. She had taken to telling stories at the library during the past year, occasionally reading a book but often simply pulling tales out of the air. Seated in front of the cluster of eager young listeners, she would reach into the air and grasp an invisible story. "Look!" she would exclaim, holding out her empty palm for them to see. "A new story waiting just for us!" The children would giggle and wait for whatever Mist pulled from her imagination that day. Therefore it was not unusual at this time of year for precious ornaments crafted by the children to show up on the hotel doorstep.

"Would you like some tea or coffee?" Mist said, turning toward the continuing sound of fingers on a keyboard. "I'll be happy to bring you a cup."

Max continued typing for a good ten seconds and then raised his head. "Coffee. Black." Mist smiled and stalled before stepping away. Prompted by her stance, he added, "Please."

Allison and Kinsley descended the stairs as Mist was pouring Max's coffee at the beverage counter in the front lobby. Kinsley walked in front, her mother just behind her. Both took their coats from the lobby rack. Allison looked over at Mist. "We're off for an afternoon stroll," Allison said. "Any suggestions?"

"Absolutely," Mist said. "Take a left at the end of the front walkway and continue down the sidewalk until you come to the candy shop. Marge makes the most wonderful fudge. I recommend the white chocolate with peppermint. She makes delicious caramels too. Betty is addicted to them."

"We should try both!" Kinsley looked up at her mother, face beaming.

"We'll get something to share," Allison said. "Just one kind."

Mist watched Kinsley's smile falter, and she leaned forward slightly to address the young girl. "Marge could give you small portions. Maybe you and your mom can try a few things. You can talk about it when you get there." She straightened up and continued. "Then continue on to the gallery on the corner of the next block. Clive has an impressive showing of jewelry and art. You can even sort through local gravel and see if you find a sapphire."

"A big one?" Kinsley asked.

Mist smiled. "Maybe a little one. Or maybe none at all. But the fun is in trying."

"Is there a library close by? We accidentally left the books we intended to read at home." Allison pulled gloves on and handed her daughter a pair to put on as well.

"Our town librarian, Millie, will have the library open this afternoon," Mist said. "But we have many bookshelves here in the hotel, at the back of the parlor. You're welcome to each choose something to read."

"Thank you," Allison said. "But we need two copies of the same book. We read books at the same time so we can discuss them."

"I see," Mist said, noting that Kinsley was looking down and shuffling her feet. "Well, visiting a library is always wonderful. It will be closed tomorrow and the next day, so I would definitely stop in there this afternoon. Perhaps reverse the order of your walk. The library is just past the gallery. You can choose books, then visit the gallery, and then pick up something sweet at Marge's candy shop on your way back. Tell Millie you're staying with us here at the hotel and she'll do a special guest check-out. We can return the books later for you."

"Perfect," Allison said. She prompted Kinsley toward the door, and the two left the hotel. Mist finished pouring the coffee and took it to the front parlor. Seeing Max focused on his laptop again, she set it down gently on the table beside him and returned to the kitchen, where she found Betty sorting mittens on the center island.

"The gloves for the Winter Warmth project are done!" Mist exclaimed. "They look wonderful."

"Don't they?" Betty beamed with pride. "We've had so much fun putting everything together."

"Such a rich variety of colors, and they have so many unique designs on the backs." Mist picked up a burgundy pair with a toy train design, another in hunter green with a chubby Santa Claus, and yet another in a rich royal blue with a cheerful snowman.

"And look at these," Betty said, showing off others with everything from candy canes to penguins to doves with olive branches.

"They're warm and whimsical, a perfect combination." Mist smiled, impressed.

"Glenda made scarves to go with many of them," Betty said. She pulled several out of a bag on the chair beside her and laid them out on the table, matching up the colors. "There are no designs, but she added a little fringe on the ends."

"Lovely," Mist said. She moved to the stove to check the stew, which by now was filling the entire hotel with a tantalizing aroma. She stirred it and added a bit of ground pepper. "I sense a hint of sadness in Kinsley." She moved to the rolls and lifted the towels, pleased to see the yeast had done its job.

"In what way?" Betty said.

Mist searched for the right words. "Like a flower trying to open but with outer petals holding the inner petals in."

"She does tend to be quiet," Betty said. "I noticed she barely said a word at breakfast this morning. But the holidays do seem to work a little magic here. Maybe this visit will help her."

"Perhaps," Mist mused as she sprinkled sea salt and chopped rosemary on the dinner rolls and covered them again with the towels.

"How are the other guests doing?" Betty asked. "I know Nina Pereira has been keeping to herself since breakfast. It makes me happy when people know it's fine to just rest in their rooms. No need to be social unless the mood strikes them."

Mist smiled, wondering if the jigsaw puzzle she'd placed in Nina's room had anything to do with the quiet time she was allowing herself. The snowy winter village scene in the puzzle was charming. On the other hand, the items she'd planted in Max Hartman's room had so far gone unnoticed, as far as she could tell. That didn't cause her any concern. She felt confident her choices were the right ones.

"Max is working on his laptop in the front room, and Allison and Kinsley have gone on a walk to the library, gallery, and candy shop—in that order, I believe."

"I hope you told them to try Marge's caramels," Betty said.

"I did, indeed."

"Which reminds me I need to replenish my stash! I think I'll run down there now." Betty stood up and gathered the mittens and scarves into a woven basket. "Unless you need help with dinner, that is."

Mist shook her head in a move so sleight that strangers wouldn't be likely to pick it up. "Thanks, Betty. But it's a simple meal, just something to warm people up. The stew just needs to simmer another hour. The dinner rolls will go in the oven shortly before we serve. And I have a fresh green salad already prepared."

"Then I'm off to Marge's place." Betty set the basket of knitted goods on a side counter and put her jacket on.

"I would add a scarf," Mist suggested. "Look outside." She nodded toward the kitchen window. Aspen and Ponderosa pine trees swayed back and forth as repeated gusts of wind blew through the yard.

"Good idea," Betty said. "I think I'll try out one of Glenda's scarves." She debated the contents of the basket. "Purple— No, red looks more appealing… No, purple it is, after all." Betty added the additional accessory, stepped outside, and closed the door.

Mist checked the simmering pot on the stove, satisfied the heat was just high enough to continue blending the flavors of the stew. She returned to the living room to offer a still-focused Max a refill of his coffee. Retrieving a spool of red satin ribbon from a sewing chest, she walked back to the café and wrapped a simple bow around each miniature tree. She arranged place settings and stood back, a sudden feeling of peace washing over her. Although guests were scattered at the moment, she could sense they would soon all come together—whether they knew it or not.

———

EIGHT

It was a common occurrence to hear compliments after meals, and this evening was no exception. By the time guests and locals had passed through the café to partake of the offerings on the buffet, the gusting wind had grown even stronger. The warm stew filled both stomachs and souls, helping take the edge off the harsher weather.

Clive had closed the gallery in time to build a fire in the front parlor's fireplace before dinner, providing a cozy resting place for evening lounging. So it was natural for folks to saunter toward the warmth of the flames after the meal. The fact that Mist announced she'd be bringing individual servings of apple tart out shortly only served to further encourage the group to gather together.

And so it was that the two remaining and much-anticipated guests, Michael Blanton and Nigel Hennessey, a.k.a. the Professor, arrived to a cheerful scene.

"Welcome to the Timberton Hotel," Mist said, ushering them in with feigned formality. Both guests laughed, knowing they were considered family members arriving home.

"Good evening, Mist," the Professor said, mimicking her manner. "It's quite brilliant to see you again." He shook her hand, followed that with a hug that spoke of more familiarity, and then pointed up the stairs. Receiving an affirmative nod from Mist, he ascended the stairs in a spritely manner to drop his bags off in his usual room.

Michael, who had stayed back while Mist was greeting the Professor, now pulled Mist just inside the café, out of sight of the others. Pulling her close, he kissed her softly and then repeated the Professor's greeting. "It's quite brilliant to see you again," he whispered in her ear.

Mist couldn't help but lean back and laugh. "I see your collaboration with *A Christmas Carol* didn't serve to master an English accent."

"It was worth a try." Michael grinned. "You look beautiful," he added, his voice gentle.

"Thank you," Mist replied. She'd changed into a soft burgundy dress that reached just below her knees. Two long strands of Peruvian beads complimented light embroidery around the neckline and sleeves. Not wanting to wear her hair down while serving food, she'd clipped it on top of her head with a hand-painted wooden barrette. Small tendrils trailed down along her neck. The haphazard effect was one that some might pay a substantial price for a stylist to create.

"Come say hi to the other guests." Mist tugged on Michael's hand to encourage him out of the private corner of the café. "Wait until you see Clara. She has news she'll want to share with you. We have some interesting new guests this year too. It's always fascinating to see the various personalities that show up for the holidays."

"Right…," Michael said as he followed Mist into the foyer. "Like the guy on the front porch? Talking on his cell phone?"

Mist smiled, took Michael's jacket, hung it on the coat rack, and leaned closer. "We're all works in progress," she whispered.

Clive had just finished adding another log to the fire when Mist and Michael joined the group in the front parlor. He crossed the room quickly and offered Michael an enthusiastic greeting. "Great to see you. And you brought that rascal Nigel with you too, right?"

"Righty-oh," Nigel said as he popped into the room. "Yes, right it is. Indeed, I'm here. And very glad to be here too." He handed Mist a package. "Something from England for everyone," he said. She thanked him and left just long enough to place it behind the registration counter.

A series of greetings followed—Betty to Nigel as Betty entered from the kitchen, Michael to Clara and Andrew, who were sitting together on the sofa near the fireplace, Nina, Allison, and Kinsley to both Michael and Nigel, and even Max Hartman to Michael and the Professor as Max returned from his latest phone call. After the exuberant salutations calmed down, Mist served dessert and guests settled in to visit.

"I understand you're visiting from Brazil," the Professor said to Nina, who stood near the Christmas tree. Her silver hair accented the green-and-gray-floral-print dress she wore. Jade earrings and a matching bracelet pulled the look together exquisitely "It is a fascinating country," the Professor continued. "I've always wanted to visit."

"You must come sometime," Nina said. "We are a large country, so many places to see." She took a sip of tea, having declined the tart for the lighter beverage. "I am from Manaus."

"Oh!" the Professor gasped. "How I would love to visit your opera house."

Nina smiled. "Teatro Amazonas. Yes, it is *belo*… so beautiful. I go to hear the Amazonas Philharmonic whenever I am able."

"I have been there," a voice said.

Mist, catching the unexpected comment, watched as Max put his phone away and stepped closer to Nina and Nigel.

"I saw Bizet's *Carmen* there in 2014," Max said. "A magnificent theater, built by rubber barons at the end of the nineteenth century."

"That is correct," Nina said.

"And right there in the rainforest," Max said.

"Really? You live in the rainforest?" Kinsley spoke up now, earning a cautious look from her mother. "We've been studying the rainforest in school. You have over thirty million species of plants and animals."

"Not in my house," Nina said, smiling. "At least I hope not."

Kinsley grinned. "No, but in the forest."

"Yes, I believe that's correct," the Professor said.

"And you're from England." Kinsley turned toward Nigel.

"Quite right, my dear."

"I love learning about other countries," Kinsley said. "It's one of my favorite hobbies. And ice skating. And reading, of course."

The Professor nodded with approval. "All excellent. I like a good game of chess myself. I find it a challenging way to pass the time."

"Knitting for me," Nina said. "Especially shawls in bright colors. We have beautiful wool yarn in South America."

"What about you?" Kinsley said, directing her question to Max. "What kind of hobbies do you have?"

"Hobbies?" Max repeated, as if puzzled by the word. "I'd have to think about it."

"Well, you should," Kinsley said matter-of-factly. "Hobbies are fun."

As conversation continued, Mist's heart filled with joy. One of the delights of the holiday season was watching the buzz of camaraderie as guests shared stories with each other.

Mist smiled as she saw Michael in an animated discussion with Clara and Andrew, Clara's face beaming as she held out her left hand as proof of their newlywed status. Michael and Clara had grown close after the death of Clara's former husband. His warm grin showed his delight at seeing her discover new love.

"And to think that it started with a plate of cookies," Betty said as she stood next to Mist. "Well, I'll clarify that. Technically, it started as a flirtation at their church. But I bet those cookies she took him from the cookie exchange a few years ago didn't hurt."

"Now that you mention it," Mist said, "do you need help preparing for the event tomorrow? It seems more people join in every year, although I know you always have everything under control." The traditional cookie exchange had been established long before Mist came to Timberton.

Betty tapped Mist's arm in a gesture of appreciation. "Marge and Millie will both be here early." I imagine we can handle it even if we get some unexpected participants."

"I made several extra papier-mâché baskets in case more people show up than you expect," Mist said. "I'll have them all on the kitchen counter for you to distribute as needed."

"Maybe you can help by keeping Clive out of the room," Betty said, laughing.

"I heard that," Clive said as he passed by with more firewood.

"Add Clayton to that list!" Maisie had just approached, carrying a sleepy Clay Jr. in her arms. "I'm heading home. It's time to put this little guy to bed. Plus Clayton's parents arrive on Christmas Eve day, so I only have tomorrow to get ready for their visit. I'll be at the cookie exchange though. I wouldn't miss it."

"Did I hear something about cookies?" Andrew said.

Betty laughed. "Don't worry. We always make a large plate for guests. You'll find the assorted goodies in the lobby tomorrow evening."

One by one, Mist watched the guests bid each other good night. When all had retired to their rooms, she took a place across from Michael, who now sat in his favorite reading chair near the lowering flames of the evening's fire.

"It's wonderful to see Clara so happy," Michael said. "She deserves it."

"I agree wholeheartedly," Mist said.

"You know, she's possibly the second sweetest person I know," Michael said, reaching for Mist's hand.

"Really? Is the Professor first?" Mist laughed as Michael pulled her into his lap.

"I think you know the answer to that," Michael said.

Mist relaxed into his arms and let her head rest lightly against his chest. She remained there a few minutes and then lifted her head. "I have to be up early tomorrow. There's breakfast to be served plus projects to work on for Christmas Eve. I'll leave you to read by the fire. You know where the books are, in the bookcase on the far wall." She stood up and turned to leave, then paused by the Christmas tree to glance out the front window. "Look, Michael. Snow flurries have started to fall."

Michael stepped behind her, wrapping his arms around her waist and brushing his lips against her neck. "So I see."

"The guests will be delighted," Mist said." Especially Nina, who has never seen snow before."

"Ever?" Michael said. "It seems she would have had an opportunity before now."

"She hasn't traveled, aside from one trip to Portugal as a child, to visit her grandparents. She's cared for family in Brazil her whole life."

"Then this holiday will be a treat for her," Michael said. "Just like it's a treat for all of us every year. Thanks to you, Mist." He snuck another kiss on her neck, this one around the side.

Mist turned to face him. "Thanks to all of us, Michael. It's in coming together that we feel the real joy of the season."

Michael smiled. "I know better than to argue with you."

"Smart man." Mist teased him. "See you in the morning." After another sweet kiss, Mist headed for her room, leaving Michael to his reading.

NINE

A light but steady snowfall developed overnight, greeting guests as they emerged from their rooms and followed the aroma of freshly baked blueberry scones to the café. The wind had died down overnight, letting snowflakes float down softly. A light layer blanketed the ground, with promises of increasing thickness over the course of the day.

Meals were always simple on the few days leading up to Christmas. Now, one day before Christmas Eve, locals and guests came to the buffet to find what appeared to be a basic, everyday breakfast.

"Ham and eggs!" Clayton cheered as he eyed the morning buffet spread.

"Yes," Maisie said as she set Clay Jr. on a bumper seat. "A simple breakfast will allow quick cleanup before Betty's cookie exchange."

"At least it's not green eggs and ham," Clayton said, referring to the Dr. Seuss book that Maisie had been reading to their toddler lately.

"Don't be so sure about that," Clive said, laughing. "Maybe you'd better take a closer look." He'd been the first to serve up a full plate, joined shortly after that by William Guthrie. The two sat together at a table not far from the buffet.

Clayton leaned forward and inspected the scrambled eggs. "Well, what do you know? I guess I spoke too soon." Tiny green specks dotted the eggs.

Mist overheard the conversation as she brought the freshly baked scones out of the kitchen. "It's thyme," she said, smiling at the confused look on Clayton's face.

"Time for what?" Clayton said, still considering the eggs as if unsure whether or not to add them to the slab of ham he'd already placed on his plate.

"Thyme, the herb," Mist said softly. "It doesn't bite, I promise."

"Go on, Clayton," Clive urged. "The whole breakfast is delicious, and it's fun to have something similar to a breakfast at your place, only edible."

"Hey!" William Guthrie said, defending his greasy-spoon eatery in spite of his hesitance to eat there himself.

Michael and the Professor, sitting one table away, both laughed. "I've never eaten at your place, Bill," Michael said. "But from everything I've heard it's a fair statement."

"We'll go eat there sometime," Clive said to Michael. "Sometime when you're feeling brave, that is." Even Wild Bill laughed this time.

Clara and Andrew entered, with Allison and Kinsley just behind them. The mother and daughter eyed the buffet and politely moved on to pour glasses of freshly squeezed orange juice. The four took seats together at the room's larger table.

"I'll have plates for the two of you in just a few minutes," Mist said, having been watching for Allison and Kinsley's arrival. "But you might try a scone with your juice," she suggested. After receiving a nod of approval from her mother, Kinsley jumped up and took a trip to the buffet, placing four scones on a plate. Returning, she set it down in the center of the table for everyone to enjoy. Mist soon emerged from the kitchen and slid plates in front of both mother and daughter. Allison thanked Mist, recognizing the tofu and thyme scramble. Country potatoes from the buffet accompanied the eggless entrée. "Olive oil," Mist said softly to let them know the potatoes weren't prepared with butter.

"These scones are delicious, Mist," Wild Bill exclaimed. "If you share your secret recipe, I just might make some at my own café."

"I believe recipes are to be shared," Mist said. "You might need to add almond milk and flaxseed to your inventory though."

"Flax what?" Bill asked. A forkful of ham hovered midair.

Mist smiled. "I'll give you the recipe after breakfast." She glanced around the room, taking note of the diners. Seeing Nina missing, she followed a hunch and headed for the front parlor. There, as she'd suspected, Nina stood by the Christmas tree, staring out the window at the falling snow.

"It's like a scene from a dream," Nina said.

"Yes," Mist agreed. "I never get tired of watching snow fall. Each snowflake is unique. I like to think of them as tiny miracles floating down from the sky. Or wishes, perhaps."

"It must be interesting living where you have four seasons," Nina said.

Mist smiled. "It must be interesting having over thirty million species of plants and animals living in your house." Both women laughed, thinking back to the conversation about the Amazon rainforest the night before. "Come, have something to eat," Mist said, and she and Nina walked to the café, where Nina helped herself to a selection at the buffet and then took a seat with the others at the large table.

As breakfast finished up, locals and guests scattered in various directions, and Mist turned her attention to clearing the kitchen and café in preparation for the cookie exchange. Michael offered to help, suggesting the honor of Mist's company later for a snowy drive in the country as compensation. Charmed by the invitation, she protested at first, claiming he was still a holiday guest in spite of their close relationship but then escorted him to the kitchen.

"We have a new employee," Mist announced. Betty, already in the process of washing and rinsing the morning's dishes, caught on quickly and tossed Michael a kitchen towel.

"You'll have to search for the correct cupboards to put the dishes away after you dry them." Mist teased.

"No clues?" Michael quipped. "From either one of you?"

"Consider it a treasure hunt," Mist said as she turned to Betty. "And you don't need to be doing dishes," she added. "Go get ready for your event. I'll take over."

"Okay," Betty agreed, stepping away from the sink. "But make sure to keep this new guy in line." Betty headed for the door. "And I'd keep Clive out of the kitchen right now. He'll find the hidden cookies faster than Michael will find the right cupboards for the dishes. Millie and Glenda already dropped off their contributions."

"Hidden cookies?" Michael said, his eyes lighting up. "Maybe you should tell me where they are, Betty, so I can make a point of guarding them."

"Ha!" Betty said. "That's for me to know and for you to not find out."

"You're quite the comedian," Mist said after Betty left. She handed Michael a dripping plate and smiled. "Now get to work."

* * *

An enthusiastic crowd was just beginning to gather when Mist and Michael met in the lobby for their countryside drive. Peeking into the café, they could see Betty standing near the café's longest table where the baked goods would be collected and divided.

Since hosting the cookie exchange was Betty's own long-standing tradition, Mist had simply made sure coffee and tea were ready. She'd left decorating the table to Betty. A red linen tablecloth formed the background for a scene running down the middle of the table with reindeer pulling Santa in his sleigh.

Clive had cleverly hooked up lights for the display by hiding batteries underneath the sleigh itself. The result was cheerful and bright, and Betty stood justifiably proud alongside it.

Millie's peanut butter cookies and Marge's fudge were the first selections to grace the table, as they had dropped them off during breakfast. Maisie had just arrived with her lemon nut bars, excited that Clayton had offered to watch Clay Jr. at home so she could enjoy the camaraderie without interruption.

Glenda soon followed with ginger bar cookies. "Wunderbar," she announced. "That's what we call them in my family, and that's what they are: wonderful." Glenda turned as Mist brought one of the papier-mâché baskets out into the lobby. "I love those! Betty said you made them. Do we really get to use these for our cookie assortments? Would you like us to bring them back later?"

"No, please keep them," Mist said. "They're sturdy, so you'll be able to use them again in the future. You might even fill them up as a gift basket for someone else."

"Wonderful idea," Glenda said. "That's exactly what I'll do." She returned to the café as a trio of women from a local church entered, a burst of snow following them in. Each held a container of sweet treats to share. Michael held the front door open for them and then slipped outside with Mist. He closed the door securely behind them to prevent a second blast of snow from drifting inside.

"Hat, gloves, winter boots, jacket… I think I'm set," Michael said as they walked to his car. He dusted a layer of snow off the windshield.

"As am I," Mist said though her wardrobe was different from Michael's. She'd grown fond of the cape she'd found at Second Hand Sally's a month before. The swirling movement of the design reminded her of ocean waves. With a warm sweater underneath, it was enough to hold the cold at bay. Having added gloves and faux-fur hat, she looked like she'd stepped out of a scene from *Dr. Zhivago*.

"Shall we go then?" Michael opened the passenger door.

"Let's," Mist replied. She waited while Michael closed her door, circled the car, and climbed in from the driver side.

"And just where are we going?" Mist asked, tilting her head slightly toward Michael.

"I have no idea," Michael said. "Wherever we end up, I suppose."

Mist leaned back in her seat and closed her eyes. "Perfect."

TEN

By late afternoon, enough snow had fallen to create a layer fifteen inches deep, and more snow was predicted throughout the night. The wintery landscape delighted local children and young adults as their boots kicked soft powder into the air and their bundled bodies formed snow angels on the ground.

Inside the hotel, guests gathered in the front parlor where a crackling fire and warm eggnog negated the chill outside. Michael and the Professor sat near the fireplace, each reading in a favorite spot. Clara and Andrew played a game of gin rummy at a table toward the back of the room. Nina sat near the window, enchanted with the snowy scene outside, and Max Hartman thumbed through a magazine, seemingly unnerved by the lack of incoming calls due to the holiday. Allison and her daughter sat together on the couch, discussing the first chapters of a book they'd picked up at the library. Mist refilled a dish of glazed cinnamon nuts near them, not missing Kinsley's subdued responses to her mother's comments.

Retreating to begin remaining preparations for an easy evening meal, Mist found Betty already in the kitchen, arranging a tray of cookies to place in the lobby.

"Do you and Michael have any plans for this evening?" Betty asked.

"Not tonight," Mist said. "I still have projects to finish for tomorrow. We had a wonderful afternoon though."

Betty covered the cookie assortment and sat down at the center island of the kitchen to help Mist place cold cuts on serving dishes so guests could make sandwiches for dinner. A pot of roasted tomato-basil soup simmered on the stove, filling the room with a warm ambiance. The casual dinner would offer something for everyone, just enough to tide them over until the much fancier Christmas Eve dinner the next day.

"Maisie told me you took a drive out of town," Betty said as she layered sliced tomatoes and pickles side by side.

Mist smiled, remembering seeing Maisie out playing in the snow with Clay Jr. as she and Michael passed by their house. She'd waved at Clay Jr., who'd made an awkward but adorable attempt to throw a snowball at the car.

"Yes," Mist confirmed. "We took a peaceful drive along a road not far from town. It was postcard perfect, like that out of a dream: snow-covered barn rooftops and trees with powdered branches swayed with the slightest breeze."

"It sounds enchanting, just driving along, surrounded by that scenery." Betty sighed.

"We stopped beside a small lake," Mist continued. "You must know the one, out by the old rock quarry?"

Betty nodded.

"A faint ray of light burst through the clouds, causing ice crystals across the top of the water to shimmer for just a minute before the light disappeared again." Mist paused, remembering how she and Michael had stepped out of the car to watch osprey soar above the frosty landscape. Michael had wrapped his arms around her to protect her from the chilly air. She hadn't objected even though her cape was enough to keep her warm.

"And you stayed warm enough?" Betty smiled, as if reading Mist's thoughts and picturing the scene.

"I took a thermos of hot chocolate, which we enjoyed by the lake."

"And?" Betty nudged, clearly hoping for more.

"And what?" Mist said.

"You're not telling me the romantic parts," Betty said, leaning forward. "Tell me something special. For example, how many times did he kiss you?"

Mist felt herself blush, something she rarely did. Giving Betty a devilish grin, she responded. "I believe I lost count."

"That's my girl," Betty said, smiling. "Oh, I left fresh towels for Max Hartman at his request and noticed a windmill on his desk. You didn't happen to leave a Tinkertoy set in his room, did you?

"Possibly," Mist said nonchalantly.

"It's amazing, the things that come out of that closet of yours," Betty said.

"It never hurts to be reminded of the carefree days of youth," Mist said, "especially if life becomes complicated."

"True," Betty mused.

The sandwich makings complete, Mist posed a suggestion. "Let's open the café early tonight so people can come and go at their leisure. The guests are busy with activities in the front parlor, and we won't get many locals the night before the big dinner tomorrow."

"And you'll have more time later for your projects," Betty said. "I know you're planning to spruce up the trees on the tables, plus I bet you're working on those miniature paintings you always give guests on Christmas morning. That's become a lovely tradition. You know some regular guests display them at their homes, adding the new one each year." She picked up the first of several cold cut trays and carried it to the café's buffet table.

Mist followed Betty with baskets of assorted breads and rolls for the sandwiches. Guests would have options ranging from simple hummus and avocado on wheat bread to towering sub sandwiches on french rolls. She already suspected which guests would choose which combination of ingredients, just as she saw them picking and choosing ingredients for life.

"I do have plans for the table arrangements," Mist said. "But the paintings are complete, minus details that I won't be able to add until tomorrow night."

"Still getting to know the guests?" Betty asked.

"We only get a brief glimpse into their lives during the few days they stay with us," Mist said. "If we're fortunate, the holidays let us see a little more. There is magic in the air at this time of the year, you know."

Mist returned to the kitchen and pulled a tray from the refrigerator. A dozen small pottery bowls held condiments and optional additions for sandwiches including three types of mustard, grated carrots, sliced black olives, alfalfa sprouts, peppers, and cranberry relish. Taking the tray to the buffet, she set the dishes out, each accompanied by a tiny spoon or fork. She surveyed the buffet, and satisfied with the selections, she informed the guests that they were welcome to choose what they'd like at any time.

"Clive will be the last to arrive for a change," Betty said as she watched the hotel guests file in. "He's keeping the shop open late for last-minute Christmas shoppers."

"Why don't you make him a sandwich and take it down to him?" Mist suggested. "I'm sure he'd appreciate it."

"That's a wonderful idea," Betty said. "I'll do that. And I'll come back quickly to help you clean up."

Mist gave Betty a soft pat on the shoulder. "Thank you, but it's not necessary. Spend some time there. Michael's getting well trained on cleaning up. Guest or not, he insists on helping now."

Betty proceeded to make a sizable club sandwich for Clive, wrapped and placed it in an insulated bag, and added several cookies. Leaving Mist to attend to the guests, she bundled up and headed for the gallery.

Mist turned her attention to the enthusiastic crowd, watching them put together combinations as varied as the individual personalities. This was exactly what she expected. It was one reason she loved meals that those dining could create themselves.

Seeing Kinsley at the buffet alone—Allison had already made her sandwich and chosen two seats at a table for four—Mist approached.

"What book are you and your mother reading?" Mist asked. "Did you find something good at the library?"

Kinsley shrugged her shoulders. "Something Mom wanted to read."

"But not you?"

"Not really."

"So what do *you* like to read?" Mist waited, unsure what response she'd get, if any.

Kinsley took a minute to answer, as if surprised to be asked. "I love dragons," she said. "Or anything magical or books set in worlds that aren't real."

"Fantasy," Mist said. "A very popular genre. I can see how that would appeal to you. Maybe I can find a book for you. We have a few with dragons in them."

Kinsley's eyes brightened. "That would be awesome." She glanced at her mother, who was waving her over to the table. "I'd better go," she said, leaving Mist pondering the mother-daughter relationship, not for the first time.

ELEVEN

Christmas Eve morning delivered the exact landscape guests had hoped for. A light snow had continued overnight, adding a soft layer to the previous accumulation. A few flurries were still tapering off, but the sun was already showing through the remaining clouds. Mist looked out the café window at the enchanting scene. It was perfect for her plans.

With the traditional Christmas Eve dinner scheduled for that evening, breakfast was not only casual but reserved for hotel guests only. Townsfolk knew they were on their own for the day. No one ever complained; most wanted to build up an appetite for the big meal anyway. Even those staying in the hotel enjoyed simple fare from the beverage area in the front lobby. The café doors would remain closed until the evening so that additional preparations for later could be completed with ease. There was always a sense of unveiling when the café doors opened on Christmas Eve. Not seeing inside beforehand added a sense of mystery and anticipation.

"Delicious muffins, Mist," Betty said, entering the café from the kitchen. Clive followed just behind her. "I smelled them baking early this morning. You must have been up even earlier than usual."

"A little," Mist said, turning toward Betty with a welcoming smile. "I wanted to be sure the muffins were ready to put out with the coffee at six thirty."

"I love anything with cranberries," Betty said.

"Same here," Clive said. "I grabbed one as soon as I poured my coffee this morning. And that stuff on top is great."

Betty and Mist both laughed at the typical Clive comment.

"That *stuff* is a walnut crumb topping," Mist explained. "I made a few without the crumble in case any guests have nut allergies."

Clive patted his stomach. "No nut allergy here, so I think I'd better have another one." He left for the lobby, making sure to close the café doors behind him.

"So, you have big plans today," Betty said, looking around the room. Plastic tubs and cardboard boxes sat on many of the tables and chairs. "More than usual for Christmas Eve."

"I suppose you're right," Mist said, surveying the café. "Decorating, cooking, and the activity I planned for this afternoon."

"Not to mention serving the meal later. And, if you haven't exhausted yourself, visiting with guests in the front parlor tonight." Betty opened the lid of a tub near her. "Well look at this." She pulled out a red beret and tried it on. "How do I look?"

Mist pondered responses and settled on two. "Like either a female Renoir or Monet's long-lost sister."

"Monet didn't have a sister," Michael said, having just taken the liberty of sticking his head into the café.

"That's why she would be long-lost," Mist said. "Perhaps long-lost in his imagination." She smiled. "He only had one brother."

"Ah, I should have suspected you'd know your art history," Michael said.

Mist approached Michael and offered him a kiss, which he readily accepted. "You know, you're now destined to work today since you dared to enter the forbidden café this morning."

"An assignment I gladly accept," Michael said. "Though I'll warn you I'm not much use in the kitchen. But if you're serving peanut butter and jelly sandwiches tonight, I could help."

Mist glanced at Betty. "Do we have those on our Christmas Eve menu this year?"

Betty grinned, playing along. "I'd have to check the list you have in the kitchen."

"I think we'll keep you on decorations," Mist said. "And this afternoon's activity."

"Yes, I was wondering about that," Michael said. "I saw the sign in the lobby: Meet at 2:00 p.m., front lawn. And… what does optionally mandatory mean?"

"It means guests have the option to consider it mandatory," Mist said.

"So it's not mandatory," Michael said.

"Correct," Mist said. "It's optionally mandatory." She reached into the tub where Betty had found the beret, pulled out a fedora, and set it on Michael's head. "There you go. You must wear that today."

"And what if I don't want to wear it?" Michael said.

"Then you take it off," Mist said. "You choose."

Michael took the hat off and flipped it back and forth, pondering Mist's words. "Well, now it seems more appealing to wear it." He placed it back on his head.

Clive's voice joined in as he returned from the lobby, a pocket in his plaid flannel shirt suspiciously resembling the shape of a muffin. "Is it Halloween instead of Christmas?" he asked, seeing the beret on Betty and the fedora on Michael. "What am I missing?"

"I'd say you're missing a hat." Mist calmly reached into the plastic tub and pulled out a cowboy hat. Being nearly a foot shorter than Clive in height, she had to stand on tiptoe in order to set it on his head.

"Does this have something to do with that activity this afternoon?" Clive attempted a stereotypical Western cowboy accent, doing a surprisingly decent job. "I saw the sign out by the muffins."

"Several times, I bet," Betty teased.

"It could," Mist said. "Or it could not."

"Right," Clive said. "I'll see you all later. I have customers coming to pick up special orders at the gallery." He tipped his hat, returned it to the tub, and left through the front door.

"And I need to check on the decorations you have thawing." Betty disappeared into the kitchen, leaving a confused look on Michael's face.

"You have decorations *thawing* in the kitchen? Dare I ask?" Michael ran his fingers through his hair and looked around the room.

"Just a few," Mist said. "Final touches after the rest is set up. Ready to help?" Ignoring the plastic tubs, she began pulling items out of the cardboard cartons. "The tubs are for this afternoon," she said. "We can set them by the door. That will leave the tables clear for the centerpieces."

"But you already have centerpieces," Michael pointed out. "The little trees with red ribbons are great."

"Sometimes, for a special event like Christmas Eve dinner, greater than great is preferable to great," Mist said as she pulled chiffon yardage from one box. She moved to a second carton and lifted out strings of tiny lights, battery packs attached to each. A third, smaller box revealed silver sleighs about three inches long. Finally she retrieved the vase of Queen Anne's Lace from the kitchen. Just as Maisie had said, they still looked fresh for her decorating needs.

"How would you like me to help?" Michael asked.

Mist tapped the back of a chair at one of the tables. "Have a seat here." She waited while Michael sat down, making sure he faced the small tree in the center. "Now just close your eyes," she said. Giving Mist a half-amused, half-reluctant look, he followed her directions. "Now keep them closed until I tell you to open them."

Michael sat patiently while Mist placed items on the table and moved them around. "Now can I look?" he asked.

"Not yet," Mist said.

The sounds continued: metal on the wooden surface, scissors clicking together, soft rustling of fabric. Mist focused on the decorations, not feeling a need to check to see if Michael's eyes remained closed. She knew he wouldn't open them until she said to.

"How about now?" Michael said.

"Not yet." Mist smiled. Mystery added zest to life.

A few more minutes went by, filled with snipping, tapping, and shuffling. Finally Mist circled the table and stood behind Michael. "Now."

Michael opened his eyes and remained silent for a good ten seconds.

"Well?" Mist prodded.

"It's amazing," Michael said. "I don't know where you even get these ideas."

"Imagination is a deep well that we all have within us." Mist looked over the transformed centerpiece, pleased. White chiffon twisted around the base of the tree in multiple layers, tiny sparkling lights beneath it. Tufts of Queen Anne's Lace rested on the branches, giving the impression of newly-fallen snow. Three small silver sleighs circled the tree, one covering the battery that fed the miniature lights.

"The sleighs are empty," Michael noted. "I have a hunch this has something to do with the thawing decorations."

"You just might be onto something." Mist placed her hands on Michael's shoulders and kissed the top of his head.

"So what's my assignment?" Michael said.

"Oh, yes, that," Mist said. "We're going to duplicate this for every tree, at least the fabric, lights, and sleigh placement. We'll clip the flowers for the tree branches just before dinner."

"Every tree," Michael repeated, looking around the café.

"Yes," Mist said. "And I'll decorate the buffet."

"I'll help with the individual tables," Betty said, reappearing from the kitchen. Michael breathed a sigh of relief, and Mist picked up a long stretch of chiffon. Holding it over her head, she approached the serving area, the wispy fabric trailing behind her like a sail. Christmas Eve was coming together, just as she knew it would.

TWELVE

The Professor and Max both stood on the porch, staring out at the front yard. Clara and Andrew stood next to them, equally intrigued.

"It's as if aliens landed and left pods all over," Andrew said.

"Indeed." The Professor stroked his chin.

"I must admit this is even stranger than things I see every day in Manhattan," Max added. "And that's saying a lot." He'd even put his phone away to survey the odd scene.

Michael, who had just joined the group, nodded. "I've been to Manhattan before, and I have to agree."

"Wow!" Kinsley said. She emerged from the hotel and joined Clara as the three men set off to investigate. "Where did those come from?" she asked. Her mother followed and looked out at the front yard along with the others.

"I have no idea," Clara said. "Andrew and I have been playing cards. I haven't looked outside since early morning when I came downstairs for coffee. But these weren't here then."

"Like I said, pods from aliens." Andrew grinned.

"This cannot be natural," Nina said, joining the other women. A twinkle in her eye told the others she knew it wasn't.

Mist looked out from the café window, unable to hear the guest conversations but imagining them all the same. Clive, along with Clayton and his fire crew, had done an excellent job, especially in a short amount of time since the snow had been too powdery the day before for the task. Giant balls of snow now dotted the ground like scattered marbles. She watched as Andrew, Max, and the Professor walked around the yard, wondering how soon they would figure out that the number of balls matched the number of guests.

"Should we take everything outside now?" Betty said. She indicated the plastic tubs, which were still sitting in the corner of the café.

"Are the others here yet?" Mist asked.

"Millie and Glenda are in the kitchen. Marge just closed up the candy shop, so she's on her way. And Sally ran back to get something from the thrift shop."

"Then it's time," Mist said. Choosing one of the plastic bins, she took it outside through the kitchen in order to not disrupt those on the front porch. Betty followed with another tub, as did Millie and Glenda. Lining up on the sidewalk, they set each bin down but kept the lids on. Mist moved to the front walk and addressed the baffled crowd of guests.

"Your mission," Mist began, "should you choose to accept it, is to pick one large snowball and add a medium one above it. After that, you'll need to add one more, even smaller. If you complete these tasks, you'll be allowed to see inside these bins."

"We're building snowmen!" Kinsley said, clapping her hands.

"Or maybe snow women," Clara mused.

"Snow people?" Allison said.

"It can be any type of snow person you'd like," Mist offered.

Just as excited as Kinsley, Nina clapped her hands as well. "I've seen pictures of them, but I've never had a chance to build one."

"Really? Never?" Kinsley exclaimed.

"I've never even seen snow until this visit," Nina whispered.

Kinsley clasped a mittened hand over her mouth and turned her attention back to Mist.

"There is no time limit," Mist said. "Your only requirement is to have fun. We'll be serving hot chocolate on the front porch to keep you warm and energized. You may begin anytime." She spread her arms wide to indicate the snowman bases were up for grabs.

"Let's go!" Kinsley led the parade down from the porch, choosing one of the rounded bases closest to a side fence. Allison followed and started to claim the base closest to Kinsley, but Mist called her over on the pretext of asking questions about the dinner menu for that night. By the time Mist had finished, guests had chosen their positions. Allison had no choice but to take the base farthest from Kinsley, not knowing that Betty had been standing at it until the other spots were all taken before stepping away.

As guests began rolling and patting snow into medium-sized snowballs, Mist and Betty retreated to the kitchen. Betty set up a hot beverage dispenser while Mist prepared hot chocolate. Once everything was ready, they placed a folding table on the front porch, along with recyclable paper cups and lids. Peppermint sticks and tiny marshmallows gave guests options to add to their hot beverages.

"It seems to be going well," Betty said, looking around the yard. "And look, we're drawing a crowd." She indicated the sidewalk where locals were gathering to watch the activity. Several of the townsfolk waved.

"We have plenty of hot chocolate," Mist said. "And more in the kitchen to refill the container. Let's move this out to the sidewalk."

"That's a wonderful idea," Betty exclaimed. "Why put on a show without offering refreshments for the audience? And look who's here just in time to help," she added.

"What have I gotten myself into this time?" Clive said, having overheard the last statement as he joined the two women.

"A moveable feast," Mist said as she lifted the containers of peppermint sticks and marshmallows and handed them to Betty. "If you would hold that beverage container, I'll move the folding table to the sidewalk." She set the tray of cups aside on a porch chair.

Clive placed his hands on each side of the metal container and lifted it in the air. "Whoa! What have you got in this thing?"

"About fifty cups of hot chocolate," Betty said, laughing. "And I have a hunch we'll be refilling it soon too."

"If you're putting it out there, you will, that's for sure." Clive nodded to the growing crowd in front.

"Let me help with that." Michael hurried up the front steps and took the table from Mist. "Where do you want this to go?"

"Let's put it over here. Follow me." Mist picked up the tray of cups and carried it out to the front sidewalk. Michael, Clive, and Betty all followed, and soon the hot chocolate street party was in full swing. Mist nudged Michael back to the snowman project and then began filling cup after chocolaty cup for the townsfolk.

"I have plenty of peppermint sticks in the shop," Marge said, noticing the sweet addition to the hot cocoa was a hit with the crowd. She headed off to the candy store to bring more over.

"This is fabulous!" Maisie said as she took a partially filled cup for Clay Jr. and blew across the top to cool it off before handing it to the young boy. "They're almost done with the snowmen already."

"Only the bodies," Mist said, seeing that most guests were finishing the third and smallest ball of packed snow. "The personalities are yet to come."

"Those bins?" Maisie said, eyeing the plastic tubs alongside the sidewalk.

Mist nodded. "Yes. And we're just about ready for them."

Those who had finished their tasks had already come over for hot chocolate while waiting for the others. Once the yard was filled with completed snowmen, Mist turned the hot chocolate dispensing duties over to Maisie and walked over to the bins.

"You've all created wonderful snowmen, snow women, and snow people," Mist said. A round of applause and cheers followed. "Now it's time to let their individuality shine."

Murmurs of agreement circled the crowd. In spite of not knowing what they were agreeing with, most knew if Mist was in charge, it was likely to be a good idea.

With Betty's help, Mist took the lids off each plastic bin, set them aside, and motioned the hotel guests closer. She pointed to the contents. "Now it's up to you." She stepped back as curious faces looked into the tubs, and arms began holding up items.

"What fun," Clara exclaimed as she pulled several knitted scarves out of the first bin. She debated between them, finally choosing one with red and blue stripes, along with a matching cap.

"A boa!" Kinsley shouted, draping the flouncing purple string of feathers around her own neck before racing off with it.

Andrew debated his own choices, as did the other guests, all delighted to draw unique accessories from the containers. The Professor was thrilled to find a baseball cap, having become enchanted with the American sport. Even Max seemed enthused when he pulled out a top hat and found a magician's wand beneath it.

Clive and Clayton brought out a collection of branches designed to serve as arms. Millie provided carrots—some straight, some crooked—to use for noses. Sally placed the thrift shop's coat rack, already draped with strands of beads, bright scarves, and other accessories, alongside the bins. Nina perused some of the glittery selections, resulting in a secretive discussion with Sally that sent the thrift shop owner hustling back to her shop to retrieve something else.

Mist, having spent weeks stocking the bins, watched as guests dug through the selections as if searching for buried treasure, their expressions carefree as they ran back and forth. Betty and Maisie kept the hot chocolate flowing, and townsfolk took to cheering the participants on.

By early afternoon, the front yard of the Timberton Hotel looked nothing short of a snow person fantasyland. Guests stood proudly next to their snow people as Maisie took photos with her compact digital camera, promising to send copies to each person's email. Cheerfully they congratulated each other as they made the rounds to view each creation.

"I'd say that was successful," Betty said as the guests retired inside the hotel to warm up and the townsfolk headed home to relax before they returned for the Christmas Eve dinner.

"That may be the understatement of the season," Michael said. He stood next to Mist, his arm around her waist.

"It's a good thing we got some snow," Clive said as he passed by with the empty hot chocolate dispenser.

Mist simply smiled. "I knew the snow would come."

THIRTEEN

Mist moved from table to table, turning on the tiny lights under the white chiffon surrounding the centerpieces. The last-minute addition of Queen Anne's Lace to the living trees had the exact snowy branch effect she'd hoped for. Soft melodies flowed down from speakers in the corners of the café. The combination of sparkling lights and classic Christmas music set a mood of otherworldliness. As always, Mist reserved the moments before the traditional Christmas Eve dinner for herself, allowing time for reflection before the more boisterous—and very welcome—activity to come. As much as she delighted in helping form holiday memories for the guests, she also cherished this time alone.

And so she stood quietly after the tables were determined to be just right, looking across the empty room. If not for the tantalizing aromas wafting from the kitchen and murmur of voices coming from the front parlor, she might have thought herself alone in the hotel.

She'd changed into the bohemian-style red-and-black dress that she'd chosen for the evening. That alone, with its form-fitting bodice and loose, flowing skirt, was an exception to her usual casual attire. The bold floral print and slightly off-shoulder neckline made for a more elegant look than her past Christmas Eve choices. A simple black velvet choker and garnet earrings neither matched nor clashed with the silver filigree barrette that clasped her hair at the nape of her neck. On a last-minute whim of rebellion, she'd opted to wear her everyday work boots instead of the black ballet slippers she'd planned.

Each place setting had been kept simple: a hunter green placemat, white linen napkin, and silverware. Only the favor the Professor had brought from England for each person added a lovely touch of red to the otherwise snowy forest theme.

The sound of laughter from the front room pulled Mist from her meditation, and she moved to the kitchen, where Betty, Maisie, and Clive were waiting. Mist smiled as Maisie nodded to the camera she'd placed on a counter after the snow activity, a gesture that Betty noticed but didn't question.

"How is everything?" Mist asked, her voice casual, just as it might be any other night.

"All ready to go," Betty said. "The rosemary Dijon prime rib is resting, and the other dishes you prepared are warm in the oven."

"Ready to go here too," Clive said. One hand held a carving knife and the other pointed to the words on the front of his apron: Kiss the Cook. "And Betty knows how to read!" he chuckled.

"Everything is great," Mist said. "The pecan pie cobbler can go in the oven as soon as we move the food to the buffet."

"I served the bacon-wrapped dates out in the front parlor as people were gathering," Betty said. "Most of the townsfolk are already here."

Maisie laughed, adding, "And you'd think the guests were celebrities after this afternoon. Their snow people are the highlight of conversation. Nina's Carmen Miranda snow person is especially popular."

"Oh yes," Betty said. "That one is wonderful. Nina said she loved Carmen Miranda when she was growing up. I could hardly believe it when Sally ran back to the thrift shop and returned with plastic fruit for the headpiece."

"Then it's time to open the doors," Mist said. In spite of her calm nature, a rush of excitement flowed through her. Hotel guests and local residents were growing closer each year. Even first-time guests could feel the warm camaraderie. This was her ultimate desire: that all would feel the Timberton Hotel was their home away from home.

As Betty and Maisie moved the dishes to the buffet, Mist opened the café doors to an eager crowd. One by one, hotel guests and townsfolk entered the winter wonderland that had been created for their Christmas Eve meal. Oohs and aahs floated about as the hungry crowd chose seats and admired the snowy scenes displayed in the center of their tables. Many retrieved their plates and headed quickly to the spread on the buffet.

"Look!" Kinsley exclaimed, pointing to one of the silver sleighs. "It's filled with snowflakes! And I think they're..." She leaned closer, noticing their creamy texture.

"White chocolate," Mist whispered as she passed by, filling water goblets at each table. "Nondairy," she added, directing the comment to Allison. "And you'll find a chestnut-and-cashew-nut loaf on the buffet, right between the wild rice, quinoa and cranberry pilaf, and the butter lettuce and avocado salad."

"The dressing?" Allison asked.

"Lemon-shallot vinaigrette," Mist said before moving to the next table where Michael, the Professor, and Max were seated. An empty chair waited for Clive, who stood at the buffet, carving and serving the prime rib.

"You look very handsome tonight," Mist whispered to Michael. She leaned a bit closer to him than others as she filled his water goblet.

"Why, thank you!" the Professor said, having overheard the comment. He adjusted his bow tie with dramatic flair as laughter circled the group.

"What is this?" Nina asked. She held up a twisted paper cylinder at the top of her place setting, waving the bright red favor in the air.

"That, my dear, is a Christmas cracker," the Professor announced proudly. "I brought them back from England on this last trip. Usually we would open them before dinner, but Mist and I have negotiated a plan to open them later."

Clara, Andrew, and several townsfolk also sat with Nina. Mist smiled as Andrew reached out and squeezed Clara's hand. The newlywed status of the two seniors was a reminder that life was full of surprises.

"This meatloaf is delicious!" Wild Bill exclaimed from a nearby table, his plate piled high with every possible selection. "I never tasted anything quite like it." Mist glanced at Allison and Kinsley, who both giggled.

"I'm surprised you can taste anything with all that horseradish on it." Clayton smirked as he cut Clay Jr.'s food into toddler-sized bites.

"It was right up there between the roast and the meatloaf," Bill protested. "I figured it should go on both." This resulted in smiles around the room. Everyone in town knew Wild Bill was an all-or-nothing personality.

Excusing herself from multiple offers to join tables—after all, she'd taste-tested everything while preparing the meal—Mist returned to the kitchen where she found Betty and Maisie at the counter.

"You should be sitting with the others," Mist said. "I can take care of dessert."

"It's packed out there," Maisie said. "Better to leave room for others."

"I'm keeping an eye on that cobbler," Betty said. "It'll be ready to come out in a few minutes, ready to cool a bit before serving."

"The fresh whipped cream is in the fridge," Maisie added.

Mist had to admit it was true: the café was full. Each year the Christmas Eve dinner drew a larger crowd than the year before. She already saw the possible need for two sittings in the future and hoped to find a way to keep everyone together.

Betty checked the oven and removed the large pans of cobbler, setting them out to cool. She and Maisie then began a revolving kitchen door pattern of retrieving plates from those finished with the main meal. Mist lined up ramekins and placed small portions of the cobbler in each. When they were filled, she added a dollop of whipped cream on most, leaving it off for those who chose to go without.

Serving the pecan pie cobbler set up a new round of enthusiastic comments, some enjoying the name of the dessert itself. "It's a pie!" It's a cobbler!" "It's supercobbler!" Eagerly emptied ramekins soon preceded admissions that not even one more bite of anything would be possible. With satisfied stomachs, the crowd moved into the front parlor.

"And now the Christmas crackers!" the Professor announced. He held his up for others to see and turned to Kinsley. "Would you care to help me demonstrate, my dear?"

"Of course!" Kinsley said.

"Brilliant!" The Professor counted to three as Kinsley held one end of the cylindrical favor. "Now pull!" he said. With a sharp snap, the cracker burst open and trinkets fell to the floor. The other guests and townsfolk followed suit, and soon the floor was covered with tissue-paper hats, slips of paper with riddles and jokes, and small novelty toys.

"Does anyone here play piano?" Mist asked as a flurry of activity surrounded the gathering of cracker contents from the floor.

"'Chopsticks,'" Clive volunteered, resulting in a ripple of laughter.

Betty patted him on the back. "Maybe another night, Clive."

"How about the first seven notes of 'Jingle Bells'?" Andrew suggested. "I could do that."

"Those are all the same note," the Professor pointed out.

Mist moved to the closet at the back of the parlor where the sound system stood ready to add proper ambiance. She reached to start a playlist of Christmas carols as the crowd quieted down behind her but paused as a few soft notes began before she pushed the Start button. So puzzling was the sudden melody that she wondered for a second if she had started the music without realizing it. But, turning toward the room, she had her answer. Max sat at the piano, four bars into *Carol of the Bells*. Guests and townsfolk alike sat enchanted.

Clara, who was standing next to Betty, waved Mist over. "I knew he would do this," she whispered as Mist approached. "We started talking this afternoon, outside." Mist nodded as she recalled seeing Clara and Max decorating side-by-side snow people. "He used to be a classical pianist," Clara said. "Before Wall Street seduced him, that is. His words, not mine."

"He's amazing," Mist said, as stunned as the rest of the crowd by Max's outstanding technique and musicality.

"I think he misses it," Clara said. "I could tell just by the way he talked about it."

"Without a doubt," Mist said.

Max moved on to *The First Noel*, followed by *Once in Royal David's City*. By this time, a crowd had gathered around the piano, and as he began playing *Hark the Herald Angels Sing*, voices joined in. While some guests lingered in song, others mingled around the room. Nina and Kinsley stood by the front window, discussing the varying personalities of the snow people outside. Michael and the Professor fell into a verbal dissection of Charles Dickens' *A Christmas Carol*, the Professor taking the liberty of analyzing Michael's own analysis. Allison stayed with those at the piano, adding her voice to the group.

As with the past few Christmases, Clive escorted Betty to the tree. "Close your eyes," he said as he reached into the far branches. Nina and Kinsley turned from the window to watch. Mist observed from afar, already knowing what Clive had designed for Betty this year.

"Now you can look," Clive said.

Betty opened her eyes and gasped. "It's beautiful!" A silver snowflake ornament sparkled as it dangled next to the lights in the tree. The traditional Yogo sapphire that Clive always added rested just off-center for artistic effect. Betty held the ornament up for all to see and then placed it near others Clive had made over the years: a tree, a set of silver bells, a wreath, and a reindeer.

As the evening grew late, local residents departed for their own homes, stomachs and spirits filled with the satisfaction of an exquisite meal and the warmth of companionship.

"Thank you for leaving your camera," Mist whispered as Maisie left with Clay Jr. sound asleep on her shoulder. Maisie responded with a wink and a promise to retrieve it the next day.

A few hotel guests retired to their rooms; others lingered in the front parlor with mugs of hot cider or iced cranberry spritzers, depending on their inclinations. Clara and Andrew snuggled together on the sofa, and the Professor and Nina fell into a discussion of Brazilian history. Max and Michael continued a game of chess they had started in the late afternoon. And Kinsley, yawning, accepted her mother's gentle suggestion that reading in bed might be a good way to wind down after all the Christmas Eve activity. Even Betty and Clive said good night after enjoying a kiss beneath the mistletoe that hung in the entryway.

Late in the evening, Mist dimmed the lights on the empty parlor, took an afghan from the downstairs linen closet, and curled up in a wicker love seat on the front porch. In spite of the storm that had come and gone, the temperature was barely chilly. The contrast of the warm fabric wrap and cool air on her face felt invigorating and relaxing at the same time.

"Communing with the snow people?" Michael's voice and presence warmed her heart as he sat down beside her. She opened the afghan and rearranged it to spread across their laps.

"I believe I am." Mist laid her head on Michael's shoulder as he put his arms around her.

"They won't last, you know, the snow people."

"It won't matter," Mist said, smiling in the dark.

"Why is that?" Michael turned her head toward his and gave her a gentle kiss.

Mist looked back out at wintery figures, surreal under the moonlit sky. "Because the memories will last."

"I guess that's what really matters," Michael said.

"Yes," Mist said. "That is exactly what matters."

FOURTEEN

Christmas morning arrived bright and sunny yet still with a chill in the air. It was the one day of the year that breakfast was reserved for hotel guests only. Townsfolk spent their time with family at home, many still full from the feast the night before. So it was with the guests, as well, who were always pleased with the light offerings they'd find in the café.

Mist had awakened early in spite of staying up into the early morning to finish the miniature paintings for guests. The aroma of freshly brewed coffee had filled the lobby at 6:30 a.m. as always, along with that of apple-cinnamon muffins baking in the kitchen. The rest of the meal required no cooking. Clive had appeared within minutes of the coffee being set out, as he did every morning. He also built a fire in the fireplace so guests could wake up to a warm Christmas morning ambiance.

Knowing most guests would sleep in after the festivities the night before, Mist still smiled when she heard early footsteps on the stairs as she placed homemade granola and mixed berries on the buffet. She'd expected as much and was not surprised to find Kinsley in the front parlor, kneeling in front of the

Christmas tree. Presents had appeared overnight, gifts that guests familiar with each other had brought with them. Mist's additions sat tucked inside the branches, wrapped in white rice paper with hand-painted silver snowflakes. Narrow satin ribbons in varying colors would allow her to distribute the gifts to the correct guests.

Kinsley looked up and smiled as Mist entered the room. "Something from Mom," she said, holding up a package. "And I brought something for her too." She pointed to another gift under the tree.

"She'll love it," Mist said.

"But you don't even know what it is," Kinsley pointed out.

"I don't need to know," Mist said. "She'll love it because it's from you."

Kinsley sighed as she looked down at the present in her hands. "She doesn't let me do many things on my own."

"She will," Mist said. "Give her time. She was quite impressed with the snow person you decorated yesterday."

"It was really different from hers," Kinsley said.

Mist smiled. "I suspect that is part of what impressed her." She leaned closer, adding, "I loved the way you propped the straw bird on its shoulder."

"Thanks," Kinsley said.

The sound of additional steps on the stairway preceded Clara and Andrew's arrival downstairs. They wore matching red sweatshirts with the words Let it snow printed above a trio of snowflakes.

"Appropriate, don't you think?" Clara said.

"Perhaps the very reason it snowed," Andrew added, laughing.

"I don't doubt it a bit," Mist said. "Help yourselves to coffee or tea or even hot chocolate if you happened to wake up with a sweet tooth."

Clara and Andrew filled mugs with coffee and then bundled up, taking their steaming beverages with them as they stepped out to admire the snow people in the yard. One by one, guests appeared, some heading first to the light meal, others joining Clara and Andrew outside before coming in to sit by the fire. Michael looked especially handsome in a black turtleneck and khakis. He took a seat in his favorite chair, enjoying a warm embrace from Mist on the way. The Professor sat across from him, looking both festive and proper in a red argyle vest. Max joined the group last. Mist suspected he'd sent a few texts off earlier but noticed he'd put his phone away or—was it possible?—left the phone in his room.

When the guests were finally settled together in front of the fire, those who knew each other exchanged gifts. Kinsley was surprised to receive a sweater she'd dropped hints about, a style popular with her peer group, as well as a paperback copy of *The Lion, the Witch, and the Wardrobe*, which Mist had pulled from the closet and placed under the tree. Allison beamed as she held up a plate Kinsley had decorated for her in art class, and Clara and Andrew declared their present was each other.

"I have a little something for all of you," Mist said, taking a place beside the Christmas tree. "Some of you have stayed here many times in the past and already know you are considered family. To those of you here for the first time, know that you are now family too. Hopefully, we'll see many of you again. Meanwhile, we like you to take a small token of our appreciation home with you to remind you of your holiday in Timberton."

"A small token," Clive whispered to Betty. "Those miniature paintings are drawing higher and higher prices each year in the gallery."

"Hush," Betty said, patting his shoulder affectionately.

"Over the past few years," Mist continued, "I've handed these out one by one. This year will be different. You may all open them at the same time."

"Ah, they must be the same," the Professor said.

"Yes and no," Mist replied as she drew each package from the tree, checking the color of the satin ribbons and handing them to specific people accordingly.

"The snowflakes are pretty!" Kinsley exclaimed as she took her wrapped gift from Mist.

"I agree," Nina said, running her fingers over the texture of the silver paint. "I will save this paper to remember the falling snow."

"Can we open them now?" Kinsley asked, looking to both her mother and Mist.

"It's up to Mist," Allison said.

"What do *you* think, Kinsley?" Mist said. "I'll let you decide."

Kinsley stood and looked around the room, taking the responsibility seriously. Clara, Andrew, Michael, Nina. Allison, and the Professor all held their wrapped packages and waited, some fighting back smiles in mock seriousness, others giving in and grinning.

"Well?" the Professor said, tapping his foot.

"I say… now!" Kinsley set to opening her gift, as did all the others. A smile crossed every face in the room once the wrapping paper was removed.

"Why, it's my snow person," Nina exclaimed. "Not just any snow person. It's *my* snow person, Carmen Miranda!"

"And my bird lady!" Kinsley said, giving Mist a hug. "The bird looks just like the one I put on her shoulder too. It even has the little red bow I put on it."

"How about yours, Max?" Clara asked, showing off her own sweet snow woman with a fringed shawl and granny glasses.

Max held his painting up, showing the top hat, cape, and wand on his snowman.

"I believe that's a snow magician," the Professor said. "Quite brilliant."

"I loved magic as a child," Max explained. "I still do."

"Then I have a good card trick to show you," Andrew offered.

Max nodded. "It's a deal."

"Yours looks just like your snow artist," Kinsley said, directing her comment to her mother. "It has the beret you put on it and the paintbrush too. Wait… I didn't see a paintbrush in any of the bins," she added. "Where did you get that?"

Allison sent a sly look to Mist, who maintained an expression of innocence.

"Maybe it was magic," Max suggested, causing Kinsley to giggle.

Michael spoke up next. "I like your scuba diver, Andrew. I'm still amazed you were able to get those fins to hang off his arms."

"They weren't terribly heavy," Andrew explained. "But I did have to switch out my first set of arms for stronger branches."

Kinsley walked over to Michael, curious to see his painting. "I saw that little boy saying 'fireman, fireman,' over and over to you."

"Yes." Michael laughed, remembering Clay Jr.'s insistent pleading. "His father is the fire captain. He brought the hat and goggles down from the station. I added the garden hose."

"Let's line them all up together," Kinsley suggested, pointing to the top of the piano. "And then go see the real ones."

"They're framed to either stand or hang," Mist said. "So that would work."

In agreement, the guests set their paintings on the piano, creating a miniature display, and then followed Kinsley and her mother outside where they found a few townsfolk admiring the full-sized creations from the sidewalk. Betty and Clive accompanied the others, along with Maisie, who had stopped by after her own family celebration to wish everyone a Merry Christmas and pick up her camera.

Mist and Michael remained indoors, observing the activity from the front window. Gently Mist reached behind the tree and lifted up a flat, rectangular package wrapped in butcher paper. Random words and phrases swirled across the wrapping in varied calligraphy fonts and at odd angles. "For you," she said, placing the gift in Michael's hands.

"Just what is this?" Michael asked, his expression so modest and sweet that Mist blushed.

"Some old thing," Mist said casually as she watched the growing activity outside. She suspected a snowball could fly at any moment and pondered who might throw the first pitch. Hearing the crinkling sound of paper unfolding, she turned as Michael lifted a wooden frame from the wrapping.

"Mist… it's wonderful," Michael said. He held it out in front of him and then brought it closer to inspect. "Wait… It's not… I mean, you wouldn't…"

"Actually it is, and I did," Mist said. "But most of the credit goes to the Professor, not to me. He has a friend in London who deals in rare books. The gentleman received a first edition…"

"Of Dickens' *A Christmas Carol*? Chapman and Hall, 1843?" Michael's voice shook. "I see the MDCCCXLIII but…"

"Let me finish," Mist said, taking on a schoolteacher tone. "The book itself was in poor condition—poorer than poor, according to the Professor. Only this page was salvageable, and as you can see, it is fairly mangled around the edges at that." Mist pointed to multiple creases and tears beneath the protective glass.

"I'm…" Michael tried to find words. "I'm… speechless."

Mist shrugged her shoulders and smiled. "That's fine. Then just kiss me."

Not one to disobey a Christmas morning request, Michael pulled Mist into his arms, first setting the framed page aside carefully. Both ignored a snowball that hit the front window as they kissed. The sound of a throat clearing drew them apart, both grinning at the recognizable harrumph.

"Your timing leaves something to be desired, Clive," Michael said, laughing.

"We'll let Mist decide about that," Clive said as he handed Mist a box approximately five inches square. A single white ribbon tied in a bow held the lid in place.

"Why, thank you, Clive," Mist said.

"Don't thank me." Clive chuckled. "It's from this goofus over here." He stuck his thumb out and pointed at Michael. With a mock butler bow, he left to join the others outside.

"Open it," Michael said once Clive was gone.

"It must be a crystal ball," Mist mused, wrapping her hands around the box to feel the weight and size.

"You won't know until you open it." Michael said.

"As you wish." Mist moved away from the front window and sat on the sofa. Delicately she untied the ribbon and opened the box. She reached in with one hand and lifted out a silver jar with the word *wishes* engraved on the front. A tiny sapphire dotted the *i*. "It's beautiful," she exclaimed, holding the jar out to catch the light.

"Now open it," Michael said.

"I *did* open it." Mist attempted a pouting look without success, then brightened. "*Oh*, you mean open *this*..." Lifting the delicate silver lid, she set it on a side table, looked inside the jar, and tipped it over. Tiny strips of paper floated into her other hand. "They're wishes," she mused as she picked up a paper that said *joy*. Another said *sunshine*, and yet another said *peace*. "And this is your handwriting. You wrote each one of these."

Michael nodded. "Yes, because these are my wishes for you, three hundred sixty-five of them so you can have one every day."

Mist remained quiet, thinking this over. "What about leap year?" she asked.

"I'll have to think about that," Michael said teasingly.

"Do you want to know what I wish right now?" Mist whispered.

"Of course I do." Michael leaned closer.

"I wish to smother you with..." She left the sentence unfinished for effect. Jumping up, she hurried to the front door and ran outside, not even bothering with her cape. By the time Michael caught up with her, she'd already grasped a handful of snow, which she promptly smashed on top of his head. He reciprocated quickly, and in a matter of moments, a full-fledged snowball war was in progress. Andrew and Clive formed a coalition and started an exchange with Clara and Betty. Nina aimed a solid shot at Max, who first stiffened but then burst into laughter and sent a toss of his own at the Professor. And Kinsley shrieked with delight as she and her mother tossed snowballs back and forth between them.

As some of the townsfolk watched the merriment from the street, one visiting family member leaned toward a local to ask, "Is this a special gathering of some sort?"

The recipient of the question smiled as he replied. "Nothing out of the ordinary. It's just a typical Christmas holiday at the Timberton Hotel."

BETTY'S COOKIE
EXCHANGE RECIPES

Glazed Cinnamon Nuts
Peanut Butter Cookies
Norwegian Kringla
Jo's Fudge
Wunderbar Ginger Bar Cookies
Orange Sablés
Lemon Nut Cookies
Cinnamon Cookies
Chocolate Peppermint Bark
Mrs. Prager's Cry Babies
Choco-Mint Puffs
Pecan Pie Cobbler
Meringue Chocolate Chip Cookies
Eve's Apple Pecan Pound Cake
Homemade Caramel Sauce
Pumpkin Cookies
Polka Dots
Pfeffernüsse Fruit Cake Cookies
Chocolate Refrigerator Cookies
Pecan Dreams
Aunt Shirley's Oatmeal Cookies
Lone Ranger Cookies
Mystery Bars

GLAZED CINNAMON NUTS (A FAMILY RECIPE)

Ingredients:

1 cup sugar
1/4 cup water
1/8 teaspoon cream of tartar
Heaping teaspoon of cinnamon
1 tablespoon butter
1 1/2 cups walnut halves

Directions:

Boil sugar, water, cream of tartar and cinnamon to soft ball stage
(236°F.)

Remove from heat.

Add butter and walnuts.

Stir until walnuts separate.

Place on wax paper to cool.

PEANUT BUTTER COOKIES

*gluten-free and low-carb
(Submitted by Petrenia Etheridge)

Ingredients:

1 cup peanut butter
1 cup coconut sugar
1 egg
1 teaspoon vanilla

Directions:

Mix ingredients together well.

Using a teaspoon, spoon onto a cookie sheet about 2-3 inches apart.

Press with a fork that was dipped in water.

Bake at 350 degrees for 8-10 minutes.

Cool on rack and enjoy.

**Note: Holds shape better after a few hours of cooling.

Norwegian Kringla
(Submitted by Jan Knight)

Ingredients:

1 cup sugar
1/2 cup butter, softened
1 egg
1/2 teaspoon salt
1/2 teaspoon vanilla

1 cup buttermilk
1 teaspoon baking soda
3 1/2 cups flour
1 teaspoon baking powder
(Stir into flour)

Directions:

Beat sugar and softened butter together.
Beat in eggs, salt and vanilla.
Mix together flour and baking powder. Set aside.
Whisk baking soda into buttermilk.

Add flour/ baking powder mixture and buttermilk/baking soda mixture alternately into the butter mixture until well mixed. It will be very stiff and slightly sticky to the touch.

Cover and chill in the refrigerator for 24 hours or overnight. Take a small amount of dough out of the refrigerator at a time, as it will be hard to work with if it gets soft. By heaping teaspoon, roll into a ball with your fingers first, and then roll to a pencil-sized round strip on a floured pastry cloth/board.

Shape into a pretzel by crisscrossing the strip and flipping one end through the middle.

Put on parchment-lined baking sheets. Form all the kringla before putting them in oven to ease your preparation process.

Bake at 350 degrees about 10 minutes or more until bottoms are just golden and top is just set. Do not overbake! Watch closely, as oven temps and baking time may vary.

Jo's Fudge
(Submitted by Betty Escobar)

Ingredients:

2 cups sugar
½ cup milk
½ cup corn syrup
¼ cup cocoa
¼ cup butter
1 teaspoon vanilla

Directions:

Butter an 8 x 8 x 2 pan.

Mix sugar, milk, corn syrup, and cocoa in a medium sauce pan and cook on low heat to a soft boil, only stirring occasionally.

Add butter and vanilla and cook an additional 5-10 minutes. Pour into pan and let set.

**Optional: Add nuts or coconut.

WUNDERBAR GINGER BAR COOKIES
(Submitted by Robyn Seitzer)

Ingredients:

2 1/4 cups flour
1/2 teaspoon baking soda
1/4 teaspoon salt
1/2 teaspoon ginger
1/2 teaspoon cinnamon
1/4 teaspoon ground cloves

1/3 cup margarine
2/3 cup dark brown sugar, packed
1/2 cup dark molasses
1/2 cup water
1/2 cup raisins or nuts

Glaze:

1 cup powdered sugar
2 tablespoons hot water

Directions:

Preheat oven to 375. Grease a jelly roll pan.

Sift together dry ingredients and set aside.

Cream margarine and sugar with electric mixer. When light and fluffy, add in molasses.

Add dry ingredients alternately with water, beginning and ending with dry ingredients, beating well between additions.

Fold in raisin or nuts and spread into pan.

Bake 15 to 20 minutes. Cool in pan.

Glaze by mixing powdered sugar with hot water. Spread over cake. Cut into 2 1/2 inch by 1 1/4 inch bars. Store in a tightly closed container.

ORANGE SABLÉS

(Submitted by Kim Davis, from her blog, *Cinnamon and Sugar and a Little Bit of Murder*)

Originating in France, Sablés are a shortbread-style cookie with a buttery, melt-in-your-mouth texture. With the addition of colored sanding sugar, these refreshing orange cookies are perfect for any holiday.

Ingredients:

1-1/2 cups all-purpose flour
3/4 cup cornstarch
1 cup unsalted butter, room temperature
3/4 cup confectioners' sugar

1/2 teaspoon salt
1 tablespoon orange zest
1 teaspoon vanilla extract
1/2 teaspoon orange extract
1 cup colored sanding sugar

Directions:

Beat the butter in the bowl of an electric mixer set on medium speed until creamy.

Turn mixer to low and slowly add the confectioners' sugar and beat until incorporated.

Slowly add the cornstarch, flour, and salt to the sugar mixture. Beat just until combined.

Add the orange zest, vanilla extract, and orange extract and mix on low until well combined.

Divide the dough in half and roll each portion into logs, about 10 inches long.

Spread the sanding sugar onto a flat plate and roll each log in the sugar, pressing to adhere it to the dough.

Wrap each log in plastic and chill at least 8 hours or overnight.

Preheat oven to 350 degrees (F) and line baking sheets with parchment paper.

Remove the plastic wrap from the dough logs, and slice into 1/4-inch slices. Place on prepared baking sheets at least an inch apart.

Bake 10 to 15 minutes. You don't want these to brown, but pale golden on the bottom is fine.

Allow the cookies to cool on the baking sheet for 5 minutes, then transfer to a wire rack to cool completely.

Tips:

**If dough is too difficult to slice through after being refrigerated, allow to sit at room temperature for 15 minutes to soften.

**Use different colored sanding sugars on each log for holiday celebrations, such as red and green for Christmas; pink and red for Valentine's; red and blue for Independence Day; etc.

**To make ahead of time, once the dough has been wrapped tightly in plastic, you can freeze the logs in heavy-duty freezer ziplock bags for up to 2 months. Allow to defrost in the refrigerator overnight then proceed with slicing and baking as per instructions.

Lemon Nut Cookies
(Submitted by Jean Daniel)

Ingredients:

1 cup shortening
1/2 cup sugar
1/2 cup brown sugar
1 egg beaten well
1 tablespoon of grated lemon rind
2 tablespoons lemon juice
1/4 teaspoon soda
2 cups sifted all-purpose flour
1/4 teaspoon salt
1/2 cup chopped nuts   *good with walnuts, pecans, almonds

Directions:

Cream shortening until light and fluffy, add the sugars gradually.

Add the egg, lemon juice, and the rind. Mix well.

Add the sifted dry ingredients a little at a time until mixed well.
Add nuts.

Make into a roll about 2 inches round. Wrap in wax paper and
chill for at least an hour.

Cut 1/4 inch thick slices, place on greased cookie sheet.

Bake at 325 degrees for just shy of 15 minutes.

Cinnamon Cookies
(Submitted by Jean Daniel)

Ingredients:

1 cup sugar
1/2 cup shortening
1 egg
1/4 cup milk
1/2 teaspoon salt
2 cups flour
2 teaspoons baking powder
1 1/2 tablespoons cinnamon

Directions:

Cream sugar and shortening until soft. Add well-beaten egg to the milk.

Sift flour with baking powder, salt, and cinnamon. Add alternately with liquid to the sugar mix.

Drop by spoonful on greased tin.

Bake at 400 for 20 minutes. *Can be iced after they cool.

CHOCOLATE PEPPERMINT BARK
(Submitted by Faith Creech)

Ingredients:

12 oz. white chocolate
12 oz. dark chocolate
1/2 cup crushed candy canes

Directions:

Line a 9 x 12 pan with parchment paper.

Place dark chocolate in a glass bowl and melt in microwave.

Pour onto parchment paper and use a spatula to spread.

Melt the white chocolate the same way and spread over the dark chocolate, spreading evenly.

Crush candy canes. Sprinkle on top of white chocolate while still hot.

Let harden in the refrigerator for two hours. Then break into pieces.

Mrs. Prager's Cry Babies

(Submitted by Wendy Matchett)

Ingredients:

1 cup shortening
1 cup sugar
1 egg, beaten
1 cup molasses
1/2 cup hot water
1/2 teaspoon ginger
1 teaspoon cinnamon
1/2 teaspoon cloves
1/2 teaspoon nutmeg
5 cups flour
2 teaspoons baking soda
1 teaspoon salt

Frosting:

1 tablespoon butter or margarine
2 tablespoons strong coffee, hot
1 teaspoon vanilla
1-1/2 cups sifted confectioners' sugar

Directions:

Cream shortening and sugar together.

Add 1 egg, beaten.

Add molasses and all spices.

Sift together flour, baking soda, and salt. Add to mixture.

Drop by teaspoon on cookie sheet.

Bake at 400 degrees for 12-15 minutes.

Mix frosting ingredients and frost while hot.

Choco-Mint Puffs
(Submitted by Jan Knight)

Ingredients:

2 egg whites
2/3 cup sugar
Pinch of salt
1/4 teaspoon green food coloring
1/8 teaspoon mint flavoring
6-8 oz. miniature chocolate chips

Directions:

Preheat oven to 400 degrees. Cover cookie sheet with parchment paper.

Whip egg whites to soft peaks. Add sugar gradually. Add a pinch of salt & beat until stiff.

Fold in food coloring, mint flavoring, and miniature chocolate chips.

Drop by teaspoon on parchment-lined pans. Place in hot oven & then turn off the oven immediately. Do not open door until the next morning.

Store in an airtight container. Makes 2 dozen.

**Alternate method: Bake at 275 degrees for 20 minutes. Turn oven off; leave in oven with door ajar for 30 minutes. Cool. Peel off paper.

PECAN PIE COBBLER
(Submitted by Taryn Lee)

Ingredients:

6 tablespoons butter
1 cup whole pecans
1-1/2 cups self-rising flour
1-1/2 cups granulated sugar
2/3 cups milk
1 teaspoon vanilla
1-1/2 cups light brown sugar, packed
1-1/2 cups hot water

Directions:

Preheat oven to 350 degrees.

Add butter to 9x13 casserole dish and melt in oven.

Once butter is melted, sprinkle pecans over butter.

In bowl, mix flour, sugar, milk, and vanilla. Stir to combine. Don't over mix.

Pour batter over butter and pecans. Don't mix.

Sprinkle brown sugar evenly over batter. Don't mix.

Carefully and slowly pour hot water over the mixture. Don't mix.

Bake 30 to 35 minutes or until golden brown.

Meringue Chocolate-Chip Cookies

(Submitted by Sue Powers Hampshire) (makes 4 dozen)

Ingredients:

4 egg whites at room temperature (cannot be purchased in a carton at the grocery store) - cannot have a drop of egg yolk or whites will not rise)
2 cups of sugar
12 oz. bag of chocolate chips

Directions:

Preheat oven to 400 degrees.

Whip egg whites on highest speed until peaks are formed.

Gradually add sugar to mixture while still mixing.

Fold in chocolate chips.

Using small spoons, place dropfuls of cookie dough on ungreased cookie sheet.

Put cookie sheets into oven *and turn off the oven.*

Keep cookie sheets in oven overnight or for several daytime hours.

EVE'S APPLE PECAN POUND CAKE
(Submitted by Angela Sanford)

Ingredients:

3 cups all-purpose flour
1 teaspoon baking soda
1 teaspoon salt
2 cups sugar
1-1/2 cups of vegetable oil
3 large eggs - room temperature
2 teaspoons of vanilla extract

3 cups of apples (peeled, cored, and chopped) *granny smith apples recommended
1 cup pecans, toasted and chopped
1 cup sweetened, shredded coconut

Directions:

Preheat oven to 325 degrees. Grease and flour a 10-cup tube pan.

In a large bowl, combine flour, salt, and baking soda. Set aside.

Combine oil, sugar, eggs, and vanilla extract in a large mixing bowl.

Mix at medium speed until well blended.

Using low speed, mix in apples, coconut, and pecans.

Spoon batter into the prepared pan.

Bake for 80 minutes or until a toothpick inserted in center comes out clean. ***Do not open oven during baking.*

On a wire rack, cool in pan for 10 minutes. Invert onto rack to cool completely.

*Option – Add Homemade Caramel Sauce:

HOMEMADE CARAMEL SAUCE
(Submitted by Angela Sanford)

Ingredients:

1 cup packed brown sugar
1/2 cup of butter
1/4 cup of milk
1 teaspoon vanilla extract

Directions:

Bring sugar, butter, and milk to a gentle boil. Cook until thickened, usually 1-2 minutes.
Remove from heat and stir in vanilla extract. Drizzle on cake.

PUMPKIN COOKIES
(Submitted by Micki Kremenak Jordan)

Ingredients:

1 cup sugar
1/2 cup butter, softened
1 egg
1 cup pumpkin
1 teaspoon vanilla
2 cups flour
1 teaspoon soda
1 teaspoon baking powder
1 teaspoon cinnamon
1 cup chopped dates

Directions:

Mix sugar and butter.

Mix in egg, pumpkin, and vanilla.

Mix together flour, soda, baking powder, and cinnamon. Add to mixture.

Stir in dates.

Drop cookies on parchment covered cookie sheet and bake 10 minutes at 350 degrees.

Cool and frost with powdered-sugar frosting.

POLKA DOTS
(Submitted by Shelia Hall)

Ingredients:

1 (21oz) box fudge brownie mix
1/2 cup oil
2 eggs, slightly beaten
1 cup white chocolate chips

Directions:

Combine the brownie mix, oil, and eggs. Stir well.

Stir in chips and drop by rounded teaspoons 2 inches apart on greased cookie sheet.

Bake at 325F for 8-10 minutes.

Let cool before removing from pan.

PFEFFERNÜSSE FRUITCAKE COOKIES
(Submitted by Dawn Moore)

Ingredients:

1/2 cup sugar	1/4 teaspoon nutmeg
1/2 cup shortening	1/2 cup candied cherries
1/2 cup dark corn syrup	1/2 cup raisins
1/2 cup coffee	1/2 cup dates
3-1/4 cups flour	1/2 cup walnuts
1-1/2 teaspoons baking soda	2 eggs
1/2 teaspoon cinnamon	1 teaspoon anise seed
1/4 teaspoon salt	1-1/2 teaspoons lemon extract

Directions:

Combine sugar, shortening, corn syrup, and coffee in a 3-quart saucepan. Simmer 5 min. and cool.

Sift together flour, baking soda, cinnamon, salt, and nutmeg. Set aside.

Grind candied cherries, raisins, dates, and walnuts. Set aside. Add eggs, anise seed, and lemon extract to shortening mixture. Mix well.

Stir in the dry ingredients and then the fruit mixture. Blend well and chill at least 4 hours or overnight.
Shape into 1" balls with well-floured hands and place on greased cookie sheet.

Bake at 350 degrees for 15-18 min. Dip warm cookies into glaze and place on racks to set. Store in a tightly covered container.

**Sugar Glaze: Combine 1 cup sugar, 1/2 cup water, and 1/4 teaspoon cream of tartar in a small saucepan. Boil until clear. Cool. Stir in 1/2 cup sifted powdered sugar.

Chocolate Refrigerator Cookies
(Submitted by Micki Kremenak Jordan)

Ingredients:

1-1/4 cups butter, softened
1-1/2 cups confectioners' sugar
1 egg
1-1/4 teaspoons salt
3 cups cake flour
1/2 cup cocoa
1-1/2 cups chopped pecans *May be added to cookies rather than on outside.
4 oz. sweet chocolate

Directions:

Cream butter and sugar until light and fluffy.

Add egg and mix well. Whisk together salt, flour, and cocoa. Add to mixture and blend well.

Chill dough for about an hour to make easier to handle.

Mold into rolls and then roll in nuts. Wrap in wax paper and refrigerate overnight.

Slice 1/8" thick and bake on ungreased cookie sheet.

Bake in 400-degree oven about 10 minutes. Cool.

Melt chocolate and frost center of cookies.

PECAN DREAMS
(Submitted by Cecile VanTyne)

Ingredients:

2 sticks unsalted butter, room temperature
2 cups all-purpose flour
4 tablespoons granulated sugar
2 teaspoons pure vanilla extract
1 cup finely chopped pecans
1 to 1-1/2 cups powdered sugar for coating the cookies

Directions:

Preheat oven to 300 degrees
Add the butter and sugar to the bowl of a stand mixer or use a hand mixer. Mix on medium speed until combined, then mix on high speed until very light and creamy, about one minute.

Add the vanilla and mix to incorporate. Add the flour and pecans and mix just until the flour is incorporated.

Using a small cookie scoop, place a scoop of cookie dough in your hand and roll it into a ball, then place the ball onto a large, ungreased cookie sheet. Repeat until all of the dough is rolled into balls.

Bake for 30 minutes or until the cookies are just lightly browned on the bottoms. Remove from the oven.

Allow the cookies to cool for 2 to 3 minutes, then roll the cookies, one at a time, in the powdered sugar and transfer to a piece of waxed paper.

Once the cookies have completely cooled, reroll the cookies one more time in the powdered sugar. If you like a generous coating, you might need more powdered sugar.

Store cookies in an airtight container using waxed paper to separate the layers.

Aunt Shirley's Oatmeal Cookies
(Submitted by Nana Fields)

Ingredients:

1 cup of raisins
3/4 cup of hand broken chunks of walnuts
Boiling water
1/4 cup of reserved liquid from drained raisins (a little more if desired)
1 small bowl to put raisins and boiling water in
3 cups of oats, instant or regular
1 cup of flour
1 teaspoon of salt
1/2 teaspoon of baking soda
3/4 cup of shortening
1 egg
2 teaspoons of real vanilla extract
1 cup of firmly packed brown sugar
1/2 cup of granulated sugar

Directions:

Preheat oven to 350 degrees.

Grease cookie sheet or use parchment paper; set aside.

Put raisins in small bowl and cover with boiling water; let stand for 5 minutes, then drain. Reserve drained liquid from raisins for later use.

In a bowl, mix together oats, flour, salt and baking soda. Set aside.

In a large bowl, beat together brown sugar, granulated sugar, egg, 1/4 cup of reserved liquid drained from raisins, vanilla until very creamy. May do by hand or use a mixer.

Slowly stir in dry ingredients until thoroughly mixed. Stir in raisins and nuts until evenly mixed.

Drop mounded teaspoonfuls onto prepared cookie sheet and bake for about 12 to 15 minutes or until done but still soft. Don't overbake.

Let stand for 2 minutes and transfer cookies to wire cooling rack. Ovens may vary so check on cookies the first time you make them.

LONE RANGER COOKIES
(Submitted by Cinda Unruh)

Ingredients:

2 cups flour
1 teaspoon baking powder
1 teaspoon baking soda
1/2 teaspoon salt
1 cup shortening
1 cup sugar
1 cup packed brown sugar
1 teaspoon vanilla
3 eggs
3/4 cup wheat germ
3/4 cup cornflakes
1-3/4 cups crispy rice cereal
1-3/4 cups oatmeal

Directions:

Sift together flour, baking powder, baking soda, and salt. Set aside.

Mix together shortening, sugar, and brown sugar. Add vanilla and eggs.

Add flour mixture and then mix in wheat germ, cornflakes, crispy rice cereal and oatmeal.

Drop by rounded spoonful on a greased cookie sheet.

Bake at 350° for 12-15 minutes.

MYSTERY BARS
(Submitted by Micki Kremenak Jordan)

Ingredients:

2 cups finely crushed graham crackers
1/2 cup coarsely-chopped pitted dates
1/2 cup coarsely-chopped pecans
1/2 cup semisweet chocolate chips
1 cup sweetened condensed milk

Directions:

Preheat oven to 350 degrees.

Spray either 8x8x2 or 9x9x2 pan.

Combine all ingredients and mix evenly. Spoon mixture into pan.

Bake about 30 minutes. Cool in pan on wire rack.

Cut into bars.

**Alternate combinations:

*Use 1/2 cup chopped marshmallows instead of dates.

*Leave out chocolate chips and increase dates and pecans to total of 1-1/2 cups.

Acknowledgements

Snowfall at Moonglow would not exist without help from a great team. Heartfelt thanks go to D.A. Sarac at The Editing Pen for her expertise in polishing the manuscript. Sincere gratitude goes to Keri Knutson of Alchemy Book Covers for cover design, as well as to Tara Meyers and Lego Normarie for formatting. Jay Garner, Karen Putnam, and Carol Anderson all deserve a round of applause for beta reading and plot suggestions.

Betty's annual cookie exchange may be fictional, but the recipes are very real. So get out those holiday aprons and mixing bowls, and enjoy a few sweet treats. Thank you to the wonderful readers and authors who contributed: Kim Davis, Petrenia Etheridge, Jan Knight, Betty Escobar, Robyn Seitzer, Jean Daniel, Faith Creech, Wendy Matchett, Taryn Lee, Sue Powers Hampshire, Angela Sanford, Micki Kremenak Jordan, Shelia Hall, Dawn Moore, Cecile VanTyne, Nana Fields, and Cinda Unruh.

Above all, it is the support of family, friends, and readers that allows stories like this to come to life. I send a soft flurry of snowflakes and thanks to each and every one of you.

Recipe Notes

RECIPE NOTES

RECIPE NOTES

RECIPE NOTES

RECIPE NOTES

RECIPE NOTES